PENGUIN ⓟ CLASSIC

LA VITA NUOVA

DANTE ALIGHIERI was born in Florence in 1265 and belonged to a noble but impoverished family. He followed a normal course of studies, possibly attending university in Bologna, and when he was about twenty he married Gemma Donati, by whom he had four children. He had first met Bice Portinari, whom he called Beatrice, in 1274, and when she died in 1290 he sought distraction by studying philosophy and theology and by writing *La Vita Nuova*. During this time he became involved in the strife between the Guelfs and the Ghibellines; he became a prominent White Guelf and when the Black Guelfs came to power in 1302 Dante, during an absence from Florence, was condemned to exile. He took refuge in Verona and after wandering from place to place, as far as Paris and even, some have said, improbably to Oxford, he settled in Ravenna. While there, he completed the *Divine Comedy*, which he had begun in about 1308, if not later. Dante died in Ravenna in 1321.

BARBARA REYNOLDS was for twenty-two years Lecturer in Italian at Cambridge University and subsequently Reader in Italian Studies at Nottingham University and Honorary Reader at Warwick. Her first book was a textual reconstruction of the linguistic writings of Allessandro Manzoni. The General Editor of the *Cambridge Italian Dictionary*, she was created Cavaliere Ufficiale al Merito della Republica Italiana in 1978. She has been awarded silver medals by the Italian Government and by the Province of Vicenza and the Edmund Gardner Prize for her services to Italian scholarship and to Anglo-Italian cultural relations. She has been Visiting Professor in Italian at the University of California, Berkeley, at Wheaton College, Illinois, and at Hope College, Michigan, where she has been awarded Honorary Doctorates, and at Trinity College, Dublin. Barbara Reynolds has also translated Dante's *Paradiso*, left unfinished by Dorothy L. Sayers on her death in 1957, and Ariosto's *Orlando Furioso*, for which she was awarded the Monselice International Literary Prize in 1976, for the Penguin Classics. She is the author of *The Passionate Intellect: Dorothy L. Sayers' Encounter with Dante*.

DANTE ALIGHIERI

LA VITA NUOVA
(POEMS OF YOUTH)

Translated with an Introduction by
Barbara Reynolds

PENGUIN BOOKS

PENGUIN BOOKS

Published by the Penguin Group
Penguin Books Ltd, 27 Wrights Lane, London W8 5TZ, England
Penguin Books USA Inc., 375 Hudson Street, New York, New York 10014, USA
Penguin Books Australia Ltd, Ringwood, Victoria, Australia
Penguin Books Canada Ltd, 10 Alcorn Avenue, Toronto, Ontario, Canada M4V 3B2
Penguin Books (NZ) Ltd, 182–190 Wairau Road, Auckland 10, New Zealand

Penguin Books Ltd, Registered Offices: Harmondsworth, Middlesex, England

This translation first published 1969
13 15 17 19 20 18 16 14

Copyright © Barbara Reynolds, 1969
All rights reserved

Printed in England by Clays Ltd, St Ives plc
Set in Monotype Bembo

For Edith Reynolds who first
told me about the *Vita Nuova*

CONTENTS

7

CONTENTS

CONTENTS

INTRODUCTION

THE *Vita Nuova* is a treatise by a poet, written for poets, on the art of poetry. This is not the usual view, but once the work is seen in this light many apparent incongruities fall into place. It consists of a selection of Dante's early poems – a selection he made himself – combined with his own prose commentary. The commentary is of two kinds. First, Dante narrates the events and emotions which led him to compose each poem; then, unless he considers that the meaning has already been made sufficiently clear, he analyses the poem schematically from the point of view of its content.

The majority of the poems are directly concerned with Dante's love for Beatrice, and all of them have some bearing on this theme. He does not divulge her family name but she has been identified with Beatrice, the daughter of a prominent Florentine citizen, Folco dei Portinari, who married the banker, Simone dei Bardi, and died in 1290, aged twenty-four. The story which Dante tells of his love for her, of their first meeting in childhood, of the overwhelming and transforming emotions he experienced in her presence, of his grief at her death and his self-dedication to her memory has long been part of the European tradition of romantic poetry. The sensitivity it arouses and the centuries-old accretions of personal, literary and even religious interpretation have rendered the work an almost sacred preserve where only the initiate may enter. It is true that in some respects the *Vita Nuova* is mysterious and ineffable, but it is also, in other respects, a perfectly lucid and practical manual of exposition.

Some readers resent and many skip those sections of the commentary in which Dante indicates the divisions of the poems, feeling such matter-of-fact analysis to be an intrusion into the dream-world of ecstatic love which is conjured up by the consecrated tone of the rest of the work. It is said, for instance, that Dante Gabriel Rossetti, through whose translation

11

of the *Vita Nuova* Dante and Beatrice became part of the pre-Raphaelite movement, so disliked the paragraphs in which the poems are analysed that he could not bear to translate them and had to ask his brother, William, to undertake this part of the task for him.

The chapter on personification and allegory (chapter XXV) with its interesting evidence of Dante's knowledge of the classics and of his views on the origins of Italian poetry, is also seen as a digression. And yet, on the contrary, a paragraph (chapter XI) describing the effect on him of the salutation of Beatrice is evidently, in his view, a digression, for he feels it necessary to justify, almost to apologize for, its inclusion. This passage, the most exquisite and transcendental of the entire commentary, is not, it would seem, strictly relevant. Again and even more strangely, Dante declines to relate more than the barest details concerning the death of Beatrice. He gives three reasons for this (chapter XXVIII), the first of which is that to do so would lead him to digress from the intention of the work.

If the principal intention of the work had been to tell the story of his love for Beatrice, nothing concerning her, in her life, or at her death, would have been a digression, whereas discussions of poetics and analyses of the poems might justifiably have been regarded as intrusive. If, on the other hand, this is a work on the art and technique of poetry, then nothing concerning that subject is a digression, and in order to expound his poems Dante will relate of his experience everything that is essential to the reader's understanding of them, but no more.

If the *Vita Nuova*, like the *Canzoniere* of Petrarch, consisted only of the poems, they would lose nothing of their beauty, but our understanding and appreciation of them are greatly heightened by what Dante has chosen to tell us concerning the reality behind them. That reality is both external, relating to events, and internal, relating to emotion and imagination. Part of the originality of the work rests in the intimate and personal way in which he traces the relationship between his experience and his poetry. It should, of course, be remembered that, unlike the *Divina Commedia*, the *Vita Nuova* was not intended for the general public or, as we say nowadays, the 'ordinary reader'. It was written for fellow-poets and for friends, many of them women, who shared the sensibility and thoughts of poets.

Dante was probably about twenty-nine or thirty years old when he decided to make an anthology of his poems and explain them to an élite. On his own evidence he discussed the matter at some length with another poet, Guido Cavalcanti, who was his closest friend. The *Vita Nuova* was written principally for him and, in one important respect, in accordance with his wishes, for it was Cavalcanti who supported Dante in his decision to write the commentary in Italian instead of in Latin. This was a bold step and represents a new outlook on the potential of Italian prose. Italian poetry itself went back only about 150 years. Rules governing structure, especially of the sonnet, the *ballata* and the *canzone*, were elaborated by the Sicilian poets of the thirteenth century and by their imitators on the mainland. Conventions as to subject-matter also existed. In Dante's youth Italian poetry was almost exclusively devoted to the theme of love, its nature and its influence, and to a stylized exaltation of the beauty and qualities of the beloved. Beyond this, the territory into which Italian poets might venture remained to be charted.

Some time in the 1280s, Dante, a young man in his late teens, began writing poems in Italian. According to the custom of the day he sent them, at first anonymously, to poets who were already established, requesting them to reply in kind. One of the earliest whom he seems to have approached in this manner was a poet of the same Christian name as himself, Dante of Maiano. In the poetical correspondence which developed between them the future author of the *Divina Commedia* is revealed as an intellectual young versifier, interested in the adroit management of words and ideas and showing a cautious respect for the difficulties of his craft. Admission into the recognized circle occurred soon afterwards when he circulated a sonnet describing a dream (the first poem in the *Vita Nuova*) in which Love appears in the medieval figure of a feudal lord. He has Dante's heart in his hand and in his arms he holds a sleeping woman,* naked except for a crimson mantle cast loosely about her. Love awakens her and prevails on her to eat the heart; then, weeping, he departs with her and the dream comes to an end.

Several poets sent back sonnets interpreting the dream. Dante of Maiano's was jocose and coarse, but among the serious replies was one from Cavalcanti, and this, says Dante, was the beginning of their friendship. This relationship was of the greatest importance for Dante's apprenticeship as a poet. Guido was Dante's senior by some ten years, a member of a powerful Guelf family and a man of proud and disdainful intellect. It must have been a heady and encouraging experience for the young, unknown aspirant to be admitted to his friendship. The father of Guido was an Epicurean and Guido himself had the reputation of being an unbeliever. Sombre by temperament and capable of violence, he was a member of the more militant section of the White Guelfs, an adherence which led to his death.

In his poems, Cavalcanti strives to analyse the nature of love in relation to psychology, setting forth the inherent tensions between the real and the ideal, between the senses and the mind, which render the experience destructive and disintegrating rather than joyful and fulfilling. His was a brilliant, subtle and complex mind. As a companion to Dante the full range of his influence, both formative and as a catalyst, can only be inferred, but there is enough evidence in the *Vita Nuova* to show that Dante felt deeply indebted to him. He is his 'primo amico', his closest friend, the *alter ego* with whom he discusses love, poetry and life. The symbolic dialogues in the work between Dante and the Lord of Love may well echo real conversations which he had held with Cavalcanti. There may even be something of their companionship reflected in the relationship between Dante and Virgil in the story of the

---

* Identified as Beatrice in the prose commentary.

Divina Commedia. It is, of course, undeniable that he had over-taken Cavalcanti by then in his poetic powers and in the range and depth of his vision; even in the *Vita Nuova*, from the first *canzone* onwards, he parts company with him in the direction which his thoughts on love are taking. Nevertheless, early friendship is an experience which makes a life-long impression. The memory of this friendship must have been rendered especially poignant, cut short as it was by Cavalcanti's death in August 1300 in consequence of political banishment to which Dante, then one of the priors of Florence, was obliged to set his hand.

Having caught the attention of the Florentine circle of poets, Dante continued to try his hand at sonnets, both the double and the single variety, and at the *ballata*. His themes were the conventional love situations inherited from the Provençal and Sicilian traditions: the torment of unrequited love, the need to keep secret the name of the beloved, the device of the screen-love to deceive the inquisitive, the vili-fication of Death personified as a pitiless destroyer of youth and beauty, misunderstandings with the beloved, intolerable ecstasy in her presence and anguished mortification at her mockery.

Though these are stock situations, the poems embodying them may have some reference to attraction felt for living women, to light-hearted flirtations or to actual love-affairs. Dante says in the *Vita Nuova* that he once wrote a poem listing the names of the sixty most beautiful women in Florence. He does not include it and says he only mentions it because the name of Beatrice coincided with the symbolic number nine. He wrote a charming sonnet (also excluded from the *Vita Nuova*) addressed to Cavalcanti, expressing the wish that he and Guido and Lapo (another poet-friend) might sail away in a boat, in which Merlin by his enchantment might place Giovanna, whom Guido loved, and Lagia, whom Lapo loved, and one other 'who is associated with the number thirty'. We do not know her name, but it is certainly not Beatrice.

As he proceeded Dante found that those of his poems which

departed from or extended the conventions were the ones inspired by his thoughts and feelings concerning Beatrice. A moment of crisis in their relations seems to have revealed to him both the reality of his situation and his future course as a poet. In chapter xiv he relates that he was taken to a wedding where Beatrice was present with a group of other women. Not expecting to see her, he was seized with faintness and leant against the wall of the room to steady himself. In his mortification it seemed to him that the women, Beatrice included, were making fun of him. When he later met some of them, at another social gathering, they questioned him about his love, saying, 'What is the point of it, since you are overcome in the presence of the one you love?' In the conversation which develops (chapter xviii) Dante experiences an instant of piercing clarification: both his love *and* his poetry have reached a turning-point. From now on he will find peace of mind in contemplating the beauty and goodness of Beatrice; from now on his poems will be poems of praise concerning her and all her radiant virtues.

Dante realizes, almost at once, that he has entered a new dimension. Like every artist, like every inventor or discoverer, he lingers for a moment on the threshold, wondering if his powers are equal to the new task ahead:

Reflecting deeply on this, it seemed to me that I had undertaken too lofty a theme for my powers, so much so that I was afraid to enter upon it; and so I remained for several days desiring to write and afraid to begin.

It was a turning-point not only for Dante but also for European poetry. The *canzone* which followed, the first and most famous of the praise-poems, opened up vistas and depths in which the human experience of love was glimpsed as being ultimately one with the power by which the universe is governed. Only after this *canzone* was the final canto of *Paradiso* possible.

The *Vita Nuova* is important not only because of the works which followed it but also in itself, as a guide to the poems it contains. Looking back, after the death of Beatrice, and after a visionary revelation of all that she signified, Dante felt impelled to clarify the means by which he had already extended the range of Italian poetry and by which it was now certain he would venture still farther. What innovations had he made? Not in structure: he used mainly the sonnet, *ballata* and *canzone*, in accordance with metrical rules already laid down by his predecessors. Not in vocabulary: his word-list in the *Vita Nuova* is not extensive and there is much repetition. It was in the gradually increasing admittance of reality into the enclosed garden of poetic convention that Dante made his most original and creative discoveries. This is perhaps what he means when in Canto XXIV of the *Purgatorio* he converses with the soul of Bonagiunta, the poet of Lucca, who asks Dante if he is the one who 'drew forth the new poetry' by means of the first *canzone* of the *Vita Nuova*. Dante replies: 'I am one who when Love inspires me pay heed, and as he inwardly dictates, thus do I write.' Bonagiunta answers: 'Now I see what held other poets back from attaining the "sweet new style"★ of which I have heard.' In other words, Dante had learnt to draw directly on experience.

The experience which went to the making of the poems of the *Vita Nuova* is narrated in the prose. It is not all objective experience and it has, of course, undergone imaginative and symbolic metabolism. It must be remembered that in writing the prose he is thinking *back from* the poems and it is to be expected that he will rearrange the past a little. It is also artistically appropriate to the harmony of the work as a whole that something of the distilled and rarefied quality of the poetry should be transmitted to the tone and style of the narrative. He seems to be saying: 'These are the thoughts and feelings from which I made my poem, and these are the events which gave rise to such thoughts and feelings.' From the schematic analyses which are also provided, in addition to the narrative, it would appear that Dante's method of composition included an intermediate stage in which he linked together the

★ *dolce stil nuovo*. There was both a sweet style, *dolce*, and a harsh style, *aspro*. The emphasis here is on *nuovo* (new) (*Purgatorio* XXIV, ll. 49–57).

elements of the rational discourse which was to form the content of the poem. This would be perfectly in keeping with the mental habits of a medieval poet trained in rhetoric. What is interesting is that he evidently thinks it necessary to make clear to fellow-poets and instructed readers where the content-divisions occur. Perhaps he considered that preoccupation with the *form* of poetry or with its embellishments was tending to obscure lucidity of thought.

These severely arid analyses of his poems, so much disliked by Rossetti, are really an invitation by Dante to enter his study and stand beside him while he runs a finger down the parchment page of his manuscript. 'Look,' he seems to be saying, 'here is a *canzone*. You know, of course, how a *canzone* is constructed metrically, consisting of a sequence of identical stanzas, each stanza being composed of a *frons*, which is divided into two *pedes*, and a *sirima*, which is divided into two *voltae*. What I want you to notice is the articulation of the thought-content, for this is by no means always identical with the structural articulation …' and so he proceeds, as in chapter XIX, for instance, 'so that the *canzone* may be well understood', to divide it minutely, first into three main parts, and then each of these three into subsections. And even then he says he has not exhausted all the poem's subdivisions, 'but if anyone has not the wit to understand it with the help of the divisions already made he had best leave it alone'.

Concentration on the poem's discourse, to the exclusion of its other aspects, seemed to Dante a way of unlocking more and more of its meaning. But this is to look at the matter from the point of view of the reader. The meaning was, of course, already there, because Dante had thus articulated his thought before committing it to metrical form and harmoniously ordered words. This seriousness and validity of the thought-content is an important and essentially characteristic feature of Dante's poetry. He does not proceed by random association of words or images. His work is intellectually disciplined and he has no respect for poets who 'cannot justify what they say; for it would be a disgrace if someone composing in rhyme introduced a figure of speech or rhetorical ornament, and then on being asked could not divest his words of such covering so as to reveal a true meaning. My most intimate friend and I know a number who compose rhymes in this stupid manner.'*

The workshop prose of the analytical sections is in astringent contrast with the prose of the narrative. This is heightened, sometimes to an intensity which exceeds that of the poems themselves, by a process of interpretation, whereby what might have been a matter-of-fact recital of facts and events is 'rendered' to provide preparation for the mood and style of the poetry. If, in accordance with Dante's procedure as regards poetry, we divest his prose of figures of speech and rhetorical ornament, what is the meaning revealed beneath such covering?

It seems to be as follows. Dante and Beatrice first met in childhood when she was just turned eight and he was nearly nine. He recalls that she was dressed in soft crimson and wore a girdle about her waist. Looking back on this meeting he is aware that he then fell in love with her and thought of her as angelic, endowed with divine qualities, noble and praise-worthy in all her ways. He often went where he could see her, even during his boyhood, but she does not seem to have spoken directly to him, or in a way that had particular meaning for him, until nine years had passed. Then one afternoon he saw her, dressed in white, walking down a street in Florence, in the company of two older women, and she turned and greeted him. Her greeting filled him with intense joy and he withdrew to his apartment to think about her. Falling asleep he had the dream which is the subject of the first sonnet.†

From then onwards Dante's thoughts dwelt constantly on Beatrice, so much so that his health began to suffer and his friends grew concerned about him. He admitted that it was

---

*Chapter xxv.

† It is unlikely that the first sonnet was written with reference to any particular person. This is probably an example of the way in which Dante uses the commentary to bend some of the early poems to the theme of Beatrice.

love that had thus reduced him but declined to reveal the name of the one he loved. One day while in church, as he gazed in the direction where Beatrice was sitting, he observed that another woman, in direct line with his vision, seemed to believe that he was gazing at her. This gave him the idea of accepting her as a screen-love, as was the convention inherited from courtly love. To keep up the illusion he wrote a number of poems to the screen-love who 'for several years and months' guided the attention of the inquisitive away from Beatrice. At last the screen-love had to leave Florence, and Dante, being later obliged to set out on a cavalry expedition, realized that he was travelling, as it so happened, in the direction of the region where the screen-love now lived. While on this journey he reached the decision to select another screen-love and returning to Florence he put his plan into operation, but with so much thoroughness that he aroused malevolent gossip and Beatrice, hearing of it, cut him in the street.

This undeserved snub caused him acute anguish, for until then his greatest joy had been to exchange greetings with her. The shock and grief seemed to have helped him to some extent to clarify his thoughts concerning the difference between constancy in love and what to others appeared to be philandering,* and he decided to try to justify himself in Beatrice's eyes by means of a *ballata* indirectly addressed to her. He does not say how it was received.

After further thought concerning the many conflicting aspects of love, which he embodied in several more poems, Dante was taken to a wedding where he suffered the mortification that has been described above. Three more sonnets resulted from his thoughts about this experience and then came the interrogation which enabled him to move forward from plaintive poems of bewildered despair to poems of praise. For several days he was unable to begin on his new theme. Then it happened that as he was walking by a stream of very clear water his tongue, almost as though moved of its own accord,

* See the mysterious dialogue between Dante and Love in chapter XII.

uttered the words: *Donne ch'avete intelletto d'amore.** He stored them joyfully in his mind and returning to the city pondered them for several days before finally writing the *canzone* of which they are the opening line.

This poem he circulated among a number of friends, one of whom asked him to define love and its operations, and he did so, with some diffidence, in a sonnet which owes a good deal, especially in regard to the concept of the 'gentle heart', to his predecessor of Bologna, Guido Guinizelli, whom he quotes in the first two lines. He then proceeded with the theme of praise, moving with heightened skill into a new phase of poetic creation. The praise theme was then sadly interrupted by an external event, the death of Beatrice's father. After the funeral Dante saw women who had been mourning with Beatrice returning to their homes. He heard them talking about her, 'saying how she mourned', and Dante in his turn was moved to tears. This episode led him to compose two sonnets in the form of a dialogue between himself and the women mourners.

Soon after this Dante fell seriously ill, suffering intense pain for nine days. As he lay reflecting on death it came to him suddenly with a searing awareness that Beatrice too would one day die. At this he went into a delirium in which he was tormented by nightmare fantasies and saw Beatrice lying dead. In his agony of grief he tried to call her name and his young stepsister, who was standing by his bed, began to weep. Other women who were tending him in his illness then drew near and tried to comfort him. It is to them that the second *canzone*, which relates the nightmare, is addressed.

One day after his illness he saw Beatrice walk down the street, preceded by Giovanna, whom Guido Cavalcanti loved. It seemed to him, as in a moment of revelation (his perceptions being perhaps sharpened by his illness and convalescence), that Giovanna was a forerunner, in her preceding of Beatrice, as John the Baptist had been the forerunner of Christ. The sonnet

* Translated here as: *Ladies who know by insight what Love is.* This is the *canzone* to which Bonagiunta of Lucca refers in the *Purgatorio*. (See above.)

which he wrote at the time is much less explicit than the prose and he explains this by saying that he previously thought it best not to reveal the full extent of his vision out of consideration for Guido Cavalcanti, whom at the time he believed to be still enamoured of Giovanna.

He again resumes the theme of praise and just as his serenity and powers of expression seem blended in perfect harmony, the blow falls. He had completed the first stanza of a *canzone*, designed to convey how the influence of Beatrice continued to affect him, when news reached him that she was dead. He does not say how she died or whether she had been known to be ill. For reasons he does not fully explain, he limits himself to showing the coincidence of the number nine with the date of her death, as calculated according to the Arabian, the Syrian and the Christian calendars, and then turns to the exposition of a different *canzone* in which he had given expression to his grief.

Soon after her death, Dante received a visit from Beatrice's brother, who was, he says, his next best friend after Cavalcanti. At his request he wrote a sonnet of lamentation and then added a *canzone*, which is complete, though it consists of two stanzas only, in which the grief of both the brother and Dante are subtly interwoven. On the first anniversary of her death, while he sat thinking of her, and drawing figures of angels on some wooden boards, he was visited by several men (he does not say who they were but infers that they were people of importance) who stood watching him as he worked. Absorbed in his thoughts, he did not notice them at first, but when he saw them he rose and greeted them, apologizing for his apparent discourtesy. This event led to the composition of an anniversary sonnet with two beginnings, from which it may be deduced that he had already composed the first four lines when the mysterious deputation arrived.

For a long time Dante grieved for the death of Beatrice. He was at the stage when a compassionate glance could still move him to tears when one day, as he raised his eyes, he saw a beautiful young woman gazing at him from a window with every manifestation of sympathy. At this sight his tears began to flow, so he withdrew, but later thought that such compassion must surely signify a noble love. He began, therefore, to compose sonnets to her which expressed the mingled consolation and accentuation of grief which her sympathy caused in him. Gradually he began to take so much pleasure in the sight of her that he reviled himself for inconstancy to the memory of Beatrice. Confusion and conflict arose in him, finding dramatic expression in sonnet dialogues, and just as his reason seemed on the point of being overthrown by his desire, he had a vision of Beatrice, as a child again, and dressed in the soft crimson in which he had first seen her. The effect of this vision was to bring on fresh fits of weeping so that his eyes became ringed with dark red patches; but the crisis, it seems, was over.

Making no transition in the narrative, Dante next relates that he saw pilgrims one day passing through Florence on their way to Rome to see the veil of St Veronica. They seemed to him so absorbed in their own thoughts and unaware of the grievous loss which Florence had suffered that he felt moved to address to them a sonnet on the subject.

The last sonnet of the *Vita Nuova* was written, Dante tells us, for two ladies of noble lineage who had sent word asking him to send them some examples of his work. He says nothing of the circumstances in which he wrote it, being content simply to analyse it and expound its meaning. It is an account of a vision of Beatrice in Heaven, apprehended only in part, for, says Dante, 'our intellect in the presence of those blessed souls is as weak as our eyes before the sun'.

It is *after* this sonnet that Dante, according to his own account, experienced a marvellous vision which made him resolve to write no more poetry concerning Beatrice until he could do so in a manner worthy of the things he had seen. And the work concludes with the famous undertaking to study to this end so that he may 'compose concerning her what has never been written in rhyme of any woman'.

How much of the foregoing account of the narrative of the

Vita Nuova is fact and how much is still 'covering'? It is impossible to tell for certain. To take an extreme view, perhaps none of it is true, but all of it is invented to serve as material for *exempla* in a manual of poetics. This seems unlikely, especially in the light of Dante's development as a poet who drew vividly on reality for the creation of his *belle menzogne*.* But whether wholly true (which is most unlikely) or only partly true, the narrative of the *Vita Nuova* was written chiefly for the purpose of expounding the poetry, which was written several years previously.

There is a mystery about the end. In the *Convivio*, a philosophic treatise in which Dante set out to write a detailed commentary on fourteen *canzoni*, he maintains that his love for the compassionate lady whom he first saw looking at him from a window (the 'donna gentile') prevailed over his love for Beatrice, as may be seen, he says, by reference to the end of the *Vita Nuova*. This discrepancy with the *Vita Nuova* as it has come down to us has led at least one commentator† to suggest that there were two versions of the work and that in the *Convivio* Dante is alluding to an earlier one, which has been lost, in which the 'donna gentile' was shown to have replaced Beatrice.

This fanciful hypothesis is not without psychological probability. There is, it may be noticed, rather an abrupt break between chapter XXXIX and chapter XL. In the former we are left with a picture of Dante, red-eyed with weeping, filled with shame at his inconstancy. Then comes the surprisingly calm and almost serene, though still melancholy, description of the pilgrims passing through Florence. The sonnet to which this is a prelude seems likewise to belong to another mood, as though a fair interval of time had elapsed. Then comes the rather hurried and uninformative first paragraph of chapter XLI. Considering the importance of the last sonnet it is surprising that Dante tells us nothing of how he came to write it. Compared with the detailed accounts of the circumstances

* Beautiful fictions.
† Luigi Pietrobono.

relating to almost every other poem in the book, the reference
to the two ladies of noble lineage is singularly unsatisfactory
and unconvincing. If Dante did indeed re-write the end, this
might perhaps account for the impression of a tale left un-
finished after chapter XXXIX and also for an alteration in pace
and in the quality of the prose in both chapters XL and XLI.
The latter, particularly the analysis of the sonnet, and chapter
XLII, seem to suggest a 'later' Dante than the author of the
work from chapter I to chapter XXXIX.

However this may be, and however much or little the *Vita
Nuova* reveals to us in the way of fact, it remains a unique
demonstration of a poet's art. This was the purpose of the book
and therein lies its originality.

THE TRANSLATION

No one who undertakes to translate the *Vita Nuova* can hope to do more than inspire a wish to read the original. This is especially true of the poetry. Since it is impossible to reproduce the beauty of the Italian, I have aimed at lucidity and strictness of form. These were two qualities to which Dante attached importance, as I have shown. In every poem I have adopted Dante's pattern of rhyme, but I have not always succeeded in avoiding a repetition of the same rhyme from one stanza to another. English is less rich in rhyme than Italian and avoidance of awkwardness or misplaced ingenuity seemed to me more important than scrupulous imitation at every turn of Dante's expertise.

The reader who would like to deepen his acquaintance with Dante's lyric poetry could not do better than to study the admirable two-volume edition and commentary by Kenelm Foster and Patrick Boyde, published by the Oxford University Press in 1967. In my revision of the first draft of my translation I have been much indebted to it.

Willoughby Hall   BARBARA REYNOLDS
Nottingham University
1966–8

LA VITA NUOVA

I

IN the book of my memory, after the first pages, which are almost blank, there is a section headed *Incipit vita nova.** Beneath this heading I find the words which it is my intention to copy into this smaller book, or if not all, at least their meaning.

II

NINE times the heaven of the light had revolved in its own movement since my birth and had almost returned to the same point when the woman whom my mind beholds in glory first appeared before my eyes. She was called Beatrice by many who did not know what it meant to call her this. She had lived in this world for the length of time in which the heaven of the fixed stars had circled one twelfth of a degree towards the East. Thus she had not long passed the beginning of her ninth year when she appeared to me and I was almost at the end of mine when I beheld her. She was dressed in a very noble colour, a decorous and delicate crimson, tied with a girdle and trimmed in a manner suited to her tender age. The moment I saw her I say in all truth that the vital spirit, which dwells in the inmost depths of the heart, began to tremble so violently that I felt the vibration alarmingly in all my pulses, even the weakest of them. As it trembled, it uttered these words: *Ecce deus fortior*

---

*Here begins the period of my boyhood. (See also Note.)

me, qui veniens dominabitur mihi.* At this point, the spirit
20 of the senses which dwells on high in the place to which
all our sense perceptions are carried, was filled with
amazement and, speaking especially to the spirits of
vision, made this pronouncement: *Apparuit iam beatitudo
vestra.*† Whereupon the natural spirit, which dwells
25 where our nourishment is digested, began to weep and,
weeping, said: *Heu miser! quia frequenter impeditus ero
deinceps.*‡ From then on indeed Love ruled over my
soul, which was thus wedded to him early in life, and he
began to acquire such assurance and mastery over me,
30 owing to the power which my imagination gave him,
that I was obliged to fulfil all his wishes perfectly. He
often commanded me to go where perhaps I might see
this angelic child and so, while I was still a boy, I often
went in search of her; and I saw that in all her ways she
35 was so praiseworthy and noble that indeed the words of
the poet Homer might have been said of her: 'She did
not seem the daughter of a mortal man, but of a god.'
Though her image, which was always present in my
mind, incited Love to dominate me, its influence was so
40 noble that it never allowed Love to guide me without
the faithful counsel of reason, in everything in which
such counsel was useful to hear. But, since to dwell on
the feelings and actions of such early years might appear
to some to be fictitious, I will move on and, omitting
45 many things which might be copied from the master-
text from which the foregoing is derived, I come now to
words inscribed in my memory under more important
headings.

* Behold a god more powerful than I who comes to rule over me
(i.e. Love).
† Now your source of joy has been revealed.
‡ Woe is me! for I shall often be impeded from now on.

III

WHEN exactly nine years had passed since this gracious being appeared to me, as I have described, it happened that on the last day of this intervening period this marvel appeared before me again, dressed in purest white, walking between two other women of distinguished bearing, both older than herself. As they walked down the street she turned her eyes towards me where I stood in fear and trembling, and with her ineffable courtesy, which is now rewarded in eternal life, she greeted me; and such was the virtue of her greeting that I seemed to experience the height of bliss. It was exactly the ninth hour of day when she gave me her sweet greeting. As this was the first time she had ever spoken to me, I was filled with such joy that, my senses reeling, I had to withdraw from the sight of others. So I returned to the loneliness of my room and began to think about this gracious person. As I thought of her I fell asleep and a marvellous vision appeared to me. In my room I seemed to see a cloud the colour of fire, and in the cloud a lordly figure, frightening to behold, yet in himself, it seemed to me, he was filled with a marvellous joy. He said many things, of which I understood only a few; among them were the words: *Ego dominus tuus.** In his arms I seemed to see a naked figure, sleeping, wrapped lightly in a crimson cloth. Gazing intently I saw it was she who had bestowed her greeting on me earlier that day. In one hand the standing figure held a fiery object, and he seemed to say, *Vide cor tuum.*† After a little while I thought he wakened her who slept and prevailed on her to eat the glowing object in

*I am your Master.
† Behold your heart.

31

his hand. Reluctantly and hesitantly she did so. A few
moments later his happiness turned to bitter grief, and,
weeping, he gathered the figure in his arms and together
they seemed to ascend into the heavens. I felt such
35 anguish at their departure that my light sleep was
broken, and I awoke. On reflecting, I realized at once
that the vision had appeared to me in the fourth hour of
the night, that is, the first of the last nine hours of the
night. Pondering what I had seen in my dream, I decided
40 to make it known to a number of poets who were
famous at that time. As I had already tried my hand at
the art of composing in rhyme, I decided to write a
sonnet in which I would greet all Love's faithful
servants; and so, requesting them to interpret my dream,
45 I described what I had seen in my sleep. This was the
sonnet beginning: *To every captive soul . . .*

> To every captive soul and gentle lover
>   Into whose sight this present rhyme may chance,
>   That, writing back, each may expound its sense,
>   Greetings in Love, who is their Lord, I offer.
>   Already of those hours a third was over
>   Wherein all stars display their radiance,
>   When lo! Love stood before me in my trance:
>   Recalling what he was fills me with horror.
> Joyful Love seemed to me and in his keeping
>   He held my heart; and in his arms there lay
>   My lady in a mantle wrapped, and sleeping.
>   Then he awoke her and, her fear not heeding,
>   My burning heart fed to her reverently.
>   Then he departed from my vision, weeping.

This sonnet is divided into two parts. In the first I
extend a greeting and ask for a reply; in the second I

convey what it is that requires a reply. The second part
begins: *Already of those hours* ... 50

This sonnet drew replies from many, who all had dif-
ferent opinions as to its meaning. Among those who
replied was someone whom I call my closest friend; he
wrote a sonnet beginning: *In my opinion you beheld all
virtue.* 55

Our friendship dated from the time he learned that it
was I who had sent him the sonnet. The true meaning
of the dream was not then perceived by anyone, but
now it is perfectly clear to the simplest reader.

IV

FROM that vision onwards my natural spirit began to be 1
impeded in its functioning, for my soul was wholly
given to thoughts of this most gracious person. In a
short time I grew so frail and weak that many of my
friends felt concern at my appearance. Many others, full 5
of malicious curiosity, were doing their best to discover
things about me which I particularly wished to conceal;
and, perceiving the mischievous intent of their inquiries,
in obedience to Love's will, who commanded me in
accordance with the counsel of reason, I replied that it 10
was Love who had reduced me to this state. I said this
because I bore so many of Love's signs in my face that
they could not be hidden. And when they asked me:
'For whom has Love thus dealt with you?', I looked at
them with a smile and said nothing. 15

V

1 ONE day it happened that this most gracious lady was
sitting in a place where words about the Queen of glory
were heard, and I was in a position from which I could
behold my joy; and between us, in direct line with my
5 vision, there sat another lady of very pleasing appearance
who looked at me repeatedly, astonished by my gaze,
which seemed directed at her. A number of people
observed this and soon began to draw conclusions, so
much so that as I was leaving I heard someone behind
10 me say: 'Look how he pines for love of her', and at the
mention of her name I understood that he was referring
to the lady who had sat in the direct line between the
most gracious Beatrice and my gaze. Then I was greatly
reassured, feeling confident that my gaze had not
15 revealed my secret to anyone that day. It was then I hit
on the idea of making this lady a screen to hide the truth;
and I pretended so well that in a short time most of those
who talked about me believed they knew my secret.
This lady was my screen for several years and months,
20 and to make it the more convincing I wrote a few little
things for her in rhyme which I do not intend to include
unless they relate to the theme of that most gracious
lady, Beatrice. This being so, I will omit them all apart
from one which can be seen to be in praise of her.

VI

1 DURING the time when this lady served as the screen of
so great a love on my part, there came to me the desire
to record the name of her who was of all women the

most gracious, and to accompany it with the names of
many other women, in particular the name of my gentle 5
screen-lady. And so I made a list of the sixty most
beautiful women in the city where the Almighty willed
that my lady should live, and I composed an epistle in
the form of a *serventese*, which I shall not include. I
would not have mentioned it except to relate the 10
wonderful thing which occurred when I composed it,
that is, that the name of my lady would not fit anywhere
but ninth in order among the names of all the others.

VII

THE lady who for so long had screened my true feelings 1
was obliged to leave the city I have mentioned and go to
a distant town. Dismayed by the loss of my beautiful
defence, I was greatly cast down, more than I would
have thought possible. Thinking that if I did not write 5
sorrowfully on the theme of her departure, people
would soon become aware of my pretence, I decided to
compose a lament in the form of a sonnet. This I will
transcribe because my lady was the immediate cause of
certain words which it includes, as is plain to anyone 10
who understands it. And so I wrote this sonnet which
begins: O *you who on the road of Love pass by* ...

> O you who on the road of Love pass by,
> Attend and see
> If any grief there be as heavy as mine.
> Hear me and then consider: am not I
> The keep and key
> Of all the torments sorrow can combine?
> Not my slight worth but Love's nobility

Did once to me
A life of sweet serenity assign.
Often behind me I would hear men sigh:
'How can he be
'Deserving of such joy beyond confine?'
All my elation now has ebbed away
Which once came flowing from Love's treasure-store,
And I, now poor,
Lack even words, and know not what to say.
And so, like those who secretly endure,
Their needs concealing from the light of day,
In aspect gay,
Within my heart I pine and grieve the more.

This sonnet has two principal parts. In the first my
intention is to call on the faithful followers of Love in
15 the words of the prophet Jeremiah: *O vos omnes qui
transitis per viam, attendite et videte si est dolor sicut meus,*★
and to entreat them to hear me. In the second part I tell
where Love had placed me, with a meaning other than
the one conveyed by the beginning and end of the son-
20 net, and I tell what I have lost. The second part begins:
Not my slight worth . . .

VIII

1 AFTER the departure of this lady, it pleased the Lord of
the angels to call to His glory a young woman of gentle
bearing who had graced the city with her loveliness. I
saw her lifeless body lying where many women were

★ All ye that pass by, behold and see if there be any sorrow like unto
my sorrow. (*The Lamentations of Jeremiah*, i, 12.)

mourning piteously over it. When I remembered that 5
I had seen her formerly in the company of my most
gracious one I could not help shedding a few tears. As I
wept I decided to compose something about her death,
in tribute to the fact that I had seen her one time with
my lady. I touched on this in the last part of the words 10
which I composed about her, as is plain to anyone who
understands. So I wrote these two sonnets; the first
begins: *Love weeps* . . .; and the second: *Death villainous
and cruel* . . .

Love weeps; so, lovers, come and weep likewise,
    And stay to learn the reason for his tears.
    Ladies lamenting piteously Love hears,
    Shedding a bitter sorrow from their eyes,
    For in a heart whose nature gentle is
    The cruel handiwork of Death appears,
    And all the world, save honour, most reveres
    In gracious womanhood in ruin lies.
How Love has honoured her now let me say:
    In his true form I saw him mourning there
    Beside her lifeless image, full of grace.
    Often he raised his eyes toward the place
    Where straightway sped the noble soul of her
    Who was a woman once so fair and gay.

This first sonnet is divided into three parts. In the first 15
I address the faithful servants of Love, calling on them
to weep, for their Lord is weeping. I say, 'Stay to learn
the reason for his tears', to induce them to listen to me.
In the second part I relate the cause; in the third I tell of
the honour which Love paid this lady. The second part 20
begins: *Ladies lamenting* . . .; the third part begins:
How Love has honoured her . . .

Death villainous and cruel, pity's foe,
  Thou ancient womb of woe,
  Burden of judgement irreversible!
Since thou my heart with cause of grief dost fill,
  Whence with sad thoughts I dwell,
  Reviling thee my tongue must weary grow.
If in the eyes of men I'd bring thee low,
  I shall be forced to show
  The evil wrongs of which thou'rt culpable.
Not that such felony is new to tell,
  But thus the wrath to swell
  In any who to Love for nurture go.
The world thou hast despoiled of courtesy
  And all of women's virtue that men praise.
  Of her gay, youthful days
The loveliness thou hast slain wantonly.
No more will I disclose who she may be,
  Except by naming her known qualities.
  Who does not merit grace
Let him ne'er hope to have her company.

This sonnet is divided into four parts. In the first I call Death by some of its true names; in the second, still addressing Death, I give the reason why I am moved to revile it; in the third, I vituperate it; in the fourth I turn to address a person left undefined, although defined in my own intention. The second part begins: *Since thou my heart* ...; the third begins: *If in the eyes* ...; the fourth begins: *Who does not merit* ...

IX

A FEW days after the death of this lady, an event occurred which made it necessary for me to leave the city I have mentioned, and travel in the direction of the region where the lady who had been my screen was now living, though my destination did not take me quite so far. I was in the company of a great many people, outwardly at least, but I found the journey so irksome that my sighs could barely relieve the anguish I felt in my heart on drawing farther and farther away from my source of happiness. And that sweetest Lord who held sway over me by virtue of my most gracious lady appeared in my imagination like a traveller, dressed in simple, humble clothing. He seemed dejected and kept his gaze on the ground, except that from time to time he turned his eyes towards a beautiful stream of clearest water which flowed beside the road on which I journeyed. Love seemed to call my name and say: 'I have come from the lady who for a long time has been your defence; I know now that her return will be long deferred and so I have brought back the heart which you gave her at my command. I am taking it to another who will be your new defence (and as he named her I realized that I knew her well). Be careful if you repeat any of what I have told you to do so in such a way that no one perceives the simulated nature of the love which you have shown this lady and which you must now show to another.' When he had said this he vanished suddenly, as though merging a great part of himself with me; and somewhat altered in my appearance, I rode on that day very pensive, sighing a great deal. Later, from these events, I began to compose this sonnet, which begins: *As I rode forth one day* . . .

As I rode forth one day not long ago,
 Pensive about my journey and distressed,
 I met Love, like a traveller, humbly dressed,

Coming along my path, forlorn and slow.
Such wretchedness his aspect seemed to show,
He might have been a monarch dispossessed.
With thoughtful steps and sighing he progressed,
His gaze averted and his head held low.
When he caught sight of me he called my name
And said: 'From far away I bring your heart,
Where it has dwelt, according to my will,
And take it a new service to fulfil.'
Then I absorbed of him so great a part,
He vanished just as strangely as he came.

This sonnet has three parts. In the first I relate how I met
35 Love and how he looked; in the second I tell what he
said to me, though not everything for fear of revealing
my secret; in the third I tell how he disappeared. The
second part begins: *When he caught sight of me . . .*; the
40 third begins: *Then I absorbed . . .*

X

1 WHEN I returned I went in search of the lady whom
Love had mentioned to me on the road of sighs. To
speak briefly, in a short time I made her my defence,
but to such an extent that too many people talked about
5 it beyond the bounds of courtesy. This often weighed
heavily on me. For this reason, that is to say, because of
excessive rumours which, it seems, were maliciously
defaming me, that most gracious being, the queen of
virtue, in whose presence all evil was destroyed, one day
10 as she passed by refused me her sweetest greeting, in
which resided all my joy. And now, departing somewhat
from the immediate subject, I want to explain the
miraculous effect of her greeting upon me.

XI

WHENEVER and wherever she appeared, in the hope of 1
receiving her miraculous salutation I felt I had not an
enemy in the world. Indeed, I glowed with a flame of
charity which moved me to forgive all who had ever
injured me; and if at that moment someone had asked 5
me a question, about anything, my only reply would
have been: 'Love', with a countenance clothed with
humility. When she was on the point of bestowing her
greeting, a spirit of love, destroying all the other spirits
of the senses, drove away the frail spirits of vision and 10
said: 'Go and pay homage to your lady'; and Love him-
self remained in their place. Anyone wanting to behold
Love could have done so then by watching the quivering
of my eyes. And when this most gracious being actually
bestowed the saving power of her salutation, I do not 15
say that Love as an intermediary could dim for me such
unendurable bliss but, almost by excess of sweetness, his
influence was such that my body, which was then
utterly given over to his governance, often moved like
a heavy, inanimate object. So it is plain that in her 20
greeting resided all my joy, which often exceeded and
overflowed my capacity.

XII

NOW, returning to my subject, I say that after such bliss 1
had been withheld from me I was so overwhelmed with
grief that, shunning all company, I went to a solitary
place where I drenched the earth with bitter tears. When
this weeping had eased a little, I shut myself in my room 5

where I could continue my lament without being heard. And there, asking pity of the Lady of courtesy and crying, 'Love, help your faithful one', I fell asleep in the midst of my weeping, like a little child that has been
10 beaten. About half-way through my sleep I seemed to see beside me in my room a young man dressed in whitest garments; from his bearing he seemed to be thinking deeply, gazing at me where I lay. After looking at me for some time, he sighed and called me by my
15 name; then he said these words to me: *Fili mi, tempus est ut praetermictantur simulacra nostra.** Then I seemed to recognize him because he called me in the way he had often called me in my sleep. As I looked at him again I saw him weeping piteously and he seemed to be wait-
20 ing for me to say something; so, taking courage, I began to talk with him as follows: 'Lord of nobility of soul, why do you weep?' And he replied: *Ego tanquam centrum circuli, cui simili modo se habent circumferentiae partes; tu autem non sic.*† As I pondered his words, it
25 seemed to me that he had spoken in a very obscure manner, so I forced myself to ask: 'Lord, what is it that you are saying to me so obscurely?' And he replied in the vernacular: 'Do not ask more than is useful for you!' Then I began to talk with him about the greeting
30 which had been denied me and I asked him the reason. He replied as follows: 'Our Lady Beatrice was informed by certain people who were discussing you that the lady whom I mentioned to you on the road of sighs had met with some discourtesy from you; and so, this most
35 gracious being, who is the contrary of all that is dis-courteous, did not deign to greet you, fearing you might

---

* My son, it is time for our false images to be put aside.

† I am like the centre of a circle, to which the parts of the circum-ference are related in similar manner; you, however, are not.

be importunate. Therefore, since your long-kept secret is in truth already partly known to her, I want you to compose something in rhyme in which you will tell of the power I have over you on her account, and how you 40 were hers straightway, ever since your boyhood. And as witness of that, call on him who knows it and say how you entreat him to tell her; and I, who am he, will gladly prove it to her. In this way she will come to know your true desire and will see how mistaken are the 45 words of those who speak wrongly about you. Make your verses a kind of intermediary, for it is not fitting to address her directly; and do not send them anywhere where she might hear them without sending me with them; adorn them with a sweet harmony, in which I 50 shall be present whenever I am required.' When he had said this he vanished and my sleep was broken. Reflecting on it, I discovered that this vision had occurred at the ninth hour of the day; and before I left my room I decided to compose a ballad in which I would fulfil my 55 Lord's commands. Later I did write it and it begins: *My Ballad, I would have you seek* . . .

> My Ballad, I would have you seek out Love
> And to the presence of my Lady bring,
> That the excuses which for me you sing
> He may by reasoned argument improve.
>
> So courteous, my Ballad, are your ways,
> That unaccompanied
> You well might venture anywhere;
> But if in safety you would pass with ease
> Seek out Love first, I bid.
> Unwise it were to go without him there,
> For she to whom these messages you bear,

As I believe, with me is so aggrieved
That in his absence being ill-received
You'd meet with coldness and the shame thereof.

Entering with Love – an embassy of two –
Begin, with music sweet,
(When you have pleaded for her clemency):
'My Lady, he who bade me come to you
This favour does entreat:
If an excuse he has, hear it from me.
Using your beauty, Love – whom here you see –
Can make him, as he wills, change countenance.
If at another, then, Love made him glance,
His heart being constant, think not to reprove.

'Lady, his heart has ever been steadfast
In homage so devout,
In all his thoughts to serve you he pays heed,
Unwaveringly yours, from first to last.'
If she remain in doubt
Let her ask Love who knows the truth indeed.
Then lastly for this favour humbly plead:
If to grant pardon should her patience try
Let her send word commanding me to die;
Not disobedient will her servant prove.

And then with Love, compassion's key, confer
(Before your leave you take)
For he will plead my cause to her with skill:
'By means of my sweet music stay with her
And for your servant's sake
Concerning him hold converse as you will.
If your request for pardon she fulfil
By her fair smile may she forgiveness show.'
My gentle Ballad, when you please to go
At a propitious moment make your move.

This ballad is divided into three parts. In the first I tell it where to go and bid it to go safely, telling it what company to take if it wants to avoid all danger; in the second I say what it must convey; in the third I set it free to go when it will, commending it on its departure to the arms of fortune. The second part begins: *Entering with Love ...*; the third begins: *My gentle Ballad ...*

Someone might object that it is not clear to whom I address my words in the second person, since the ballad is nothing other than the words I write; and so I say that I intend to clarify and resolve this doubt later on in this little book, with reference to a still more doubtful passage. Then if anyone has a doubt or wishes to raise an objection about this part, let him defer it till later, when he will understand.

XIII

AFTER the vision which I have described, when I had composed the rhymes which Love had commanded me, a number of conflicting thoughts began to contend and strive one with the other, all of them, it seemed, unanswerably. Among them were four which seemed most to disturb my peace of mind. One was this: 'The domination of Love is a good thing because he guides the mind of his faithful follower away from all unworthiness.' Another thought was this: 'The domination of Love is not good because the more faithfully a follower serves him, the more burdensome and grievous are the moments he must endure'; yet another thought was as follows: 'The name of Love is so sweet to hear that it seems impossible that it can be anything but sweet in its effect upon most things, for it is known that names are a

consequence of the things which are named, as it is written, *Nomina sunt consequentia rerum*';* the fourth thought was this: 'The Lady for whom Love holds you so enthralled is not like other women whose hearts are
20 easily moved.' Every one of these thoughts so contended within me that I became like a person who does not know which road to take on his journey, who wants to set out but does not know where to start. The only way I could see of reconciling them all was one which was
25 very distasteful to me; that is, to call on Pity and throw myself into her arms. And as I lingered in this state, I felt a desire to compose something about it in rhyme; and so I wrote this sonnet, which begins: *All thoughts within my mind* . . .

All thoughts within my mind discourse of Love
    And have among them great diversity:
    One makes me long for Love's authority,
    Another its unreason seeks to prove,
    Then sweetness, as of hope, I'm conscious of.
    Another makes me weep incessantly.
    Only in asking pity all agree,
    Trembling in fear with which the pulses throb.
And so I know not from which theme to start;
    And I would write, yet know not what to say.
    Thus in a maze of Love I'm wandering!
    And if to harmony all these I'd bring
    My enemy I must bring into play,
    And lady Pity call to take my part.

30   This sonnet can be divided into four parts. In the first I imagine that all my thoughts are of Love; in the second I say that they are all different and I describe their

* Names are the consequences of things.

diversity; in the third I say what they all appear to have in common; in the fourth I say that wishing to write about Love I do not know which thought to take as my 35 theme; and if I want to combine them all I am obliged to call on my enemy, my lady Pity; and I say 'my lady' as a scornful way of speaking. The second part begins: *And have among them* ...; the third: *Only in asking pity* ...; and the fourth: *And so I know not* ... 40

XIV

AFTER the battle of conflicting thoughts it happened 1 that this most gracious person was present where many women were gathered together. I too was taken there by a friend who thought it would give me great pleasure to be present where so many beautiful women were to be 5 seen. Hardly knowing where I was being taken, and trusting the person who in fact had brought his friend almost to the verge of death, I said: 'Why have we come to visit these ladies?' And he replied: 'To wait on them in a manner that is fitting.' The truth is that they were 10 gathered there in the company of a lady who had been married that day and, according to the custom of that city, it was their duty to keep her company on the first occasion when she sat down at table in the house of her bridegroom. Thinking that it would please my friend, I 15 consented to stay and attend on the ladies who were present. Just as I had reached this decision, I felt the beginning of an extraordinary throbbing on the left side of my breast which immediately spread to all the parts of my body. Then, pretending nothing was wrong, I 20 leaned for support against a fresco painted in a frieze round the walls of the house. Afraid that other people

might notice how I was trembling, I raised my eyes and
as they rested on the women gathered there I saw among
25 them the most gracious Beatrice. Then my spirits were
so routed by the power which Love acquired on finding
himself so close to this most gracious being that none
survived except the spirits of vision; and even they were
driven from their organs because Love himself desired to
30 occupy their noble place in order to behold her who in-
spired such wonder. Although I was anything but my-
self, I was very much grieved for these little spirits who
lamented loudly, saying: 'If this Lord had not flung us
from our rightful place like a bolt of lightning, we could
35 have stayed to behold the marvel of this lady, as all our
fellows are doing!' A number of the women present,
observing my transformation, began to be astonished
and, talking about it, they mocked at me in company
with the most gracious one herself. Then my friend who,
40 in all good faith, had been so mistaken as to bring me
there, took me by the hand, and, removing me from the
sight of the women, asked what was troubling me. Then,
when I had rested a little and my lifeless spirits had re-
vived, and those which had been expelled had returned
45 to their rightful estate, I said to my friend: 'I had set foot
in that part of life beyond which one cannot go with any
hope of returning.' Then I left him and returned to my
room of tears, where, weeping and suffering the agony
of shame, I said to myself: 'If my lady knew of my
50 condition, I do not believe she would so mock at my
appearance; indeed, I think she would feel great compas-
sion.' And while I was still weeping I decided to com-
pose verses addressed to her, explaining the reason for
my change of countenance, saying that I was aware that
55 people did not know of it and that if it were known it
would arouse compassion. I decided to do this, hoping

48

that the verses might perchance be heard by her; so later
I wrote this sonnet, which begins: *With your compan-
ions. . .*

> With your companions you make fun of me,
>   Not thinking, Lady, what the reason is
>   I cut so strange a figure in your eyes
>   When, raising mine, your loveliness I see.
>   If you but knew, Pity no more could be
>   Severe towards me in her usual guise.
>   Finding me near you, Love his weapons tries,
>   Gaining in boldness and temerity,
> And on my frightened spirits rains such blows
>   That some he slays and others flee in fear,
>   Till only he is left to look on you.
>   Hence I am altered into someone new,
>   Yet not so that I do not plainly hear
>   My outcast spirits wailing in their woes.

I will not subdivide this sonnet as such analysis is made
only in order to disclose the meaning. Therefore, since
from the account I have given of its occasion this sonnet
is quite clear, there is no need to divide it. I admit that
among the words in which I set forth the occasion of the
sonnet there are some whose meaning is obscure, for in-
stance, when I say that Love slays all my spirits, except
the spirits of vision, which survive but are driven forth
from their organs. It is impossible to explain this to any-
one who is not to the same extent a faithful follower of
Love; and to those who are it is obvious what the mean-
ing is. Consequently there is no point in my clarifying
that doubt because such clarification would be either
useless or superfluous.

XV

1 AFTER this strange transformation, an insistent thought
came to me and would hardly ever leave me. It repeatedly
took possession of me, reasoning as follows: 'Since you
take on such an absurd appearance whenever you are
5 near this lady, why do you still try to see her? Suppose
she asked you this, what would you reply, assuming that
all your faculties were unimpeded and you were able to
reply?' To this another, humble, thought made answer:
'If I did not lose my wits and were confident enough to
10 reply to her, I would tell her that as soon as I imagine
her wonderful beauty the desire to see her takes posses-
sion of me, and this desire is so powerful that it utterly
destroys anything in my memory that might rise up
against it; that is why my past sufferings do not restrain
15 me from trying to see her.' And so, stirred by such
thoughts, I decided to write something to excuse my-
self to her in relation to this insistent thought, and at the
same time explaining what happens to me when I am
near her. And I wrote this sonnet which begins: *All*
20 *thoughts of what befalls me ...*

> All thoughts of what befalls me die away,
>   Fair jewel, when to see you I draw nigh;
>   When I am close to you I hear Love say:
>   'If you fear Death, now is the time to fly!'
> My looks the colour of my heart betray
>   Which, fainting, for support leans all awry;
>   And in this tremor as I reel and sway
>   The very stones I walk on echo 'Die!'
> A sin do those commit who see me then
>   And do not comfort me in my soul's plight,
>   At least by showing that they grieve for me,

For Pity's sake which, by your mocking slain,
Is brought to life anew in the dead sight
Of eyes which have no more desire to see.

This sonnet is divided into two parts. In the first I give
the reason why I do not stop myself from seeking this
lady's company; in the second I describe what happens
to me when I draw near her. This second part begins:
When I am close to you ... This also can be subdivided
into five sections, according to the five different things
which are narrated. In the first of these I say what Love,
advised by reason, says to me when I am near her; in the
second I convey the condition of my heart as it is shown
in my face; in the third I relate how I lose all confidence;
in the fourth I say that anyone who does not show com-
passion for me is guilty of sin, for to do so would give
me some comfort; and in the last I say why people
should have compassion, that is, because of the piteous
look which comes into my eyes. This piteousness is slain,
that is, rendered imperceptible, by my lady's mockery,
which leads others who perhaps might notice this pite-
ousness to do as she does. The second subdivision begins:
My looks the colour ...; the third: *And in this tremor* ...;
the fourth: *A sin do those commit* ...; and the fifth: *For
Pity's sake* ...

XVI

WHEN I had finished this sonnet I felt the desire to write
another in which I would say four more things about my
state which it seemed to me I had not yet made plain.
The first was that I was often distressed when memory
stirred my imagination to consider the effect which Love

was having on me; the second was that frequently Love assailed me so violently that nothing remained alive in me except a thought which spoke of my lady; the third was that when the battle of Love raged within me
10 in this way, I felt impelled, all pale as I was, to go and see my lady, believing that the sight of her would give me protection from this battle, quite forgetting what happened to me when I drew near such graciousness; the fourth relates how the sight of her not
15 only did not offer me protection but finally defeated what little life I had left. That was how I came to write the sonnet which begins: *Many a time the thought* . . .

> Many a time the thought returns to me:
>> What sad conditions Love on me bestows!
> And moved by Pity I say frequently:
> 'Can there be anyone who my state knows?'
> For Love takes hold of me so suddenly
> My vital spirits I am near to lose.
> One only of them all survives in me,
> Staying to speak of you, as Love allows.
> To aid me then my forces I renew
>> And pallid, all my courage drained long since,
> I come to you to remedy my plight;
> But if I raise my eyes to look at you
> So vast a tremor in my heart begins
> My beating pulses put my soul to flight.

This sonnet is divided into four parts, related to the four matters which it narrates and, because they are ex-
20 plained above, I will confine myself to indicating the parts by their beginnings, as follows: the second part begins: *For Love takes hold* . . .; the third: *To aid me then* . . .; and the fourth: *But if I raise* . . .

XVII

WHEN I had written these three sonnets, which are ₁
addressed directly to my lady, I had said almost every-
thing about my state and I thought it right to be silent
and say no more, for I felt I had explained enough
about myself. Although from then onwards I refrained ₅
from writing verses addressed to her, I felt impelled to
take up a new and nobler theme than before. As the
occasion of finding my new theme is agreeable to hear, I
will narrate it, as briefly as I can.

XVIII

AS many people had guessed from my appearance the ₁
secret of my heart, a certain group of ladies, who were
aware of my feelings, having witnessed my discomfiture
at one time or another, had gathered together to enjoy
each other's company. As I passed by, led as though by ₅
fortune, one of them called me. She had so delightful a
way of speaking that when I had drawn close to them
and had made quite sure that my lady was not among
them, I took courage and greeted them, asking them
how I could be of service to them. There were many ₁₀
ladies present, some laughing together, others looking
at me, waiting to hear what I would say, and still others
talking among themselves. One of these, turning her
eyes towards me and addressing me by name, said:
'What is the point of your love for your lady since you ₁₅
are unable to endure her presence? Tell us, for surely the
aim of such love must be unique!' When she had
finished speaking not only she, but all the others seemed

from their appearance to be waiting for my answer.
20 Then I said to them: 'Ladies, the aim of my love was
once the greeting of one of whom perhaps you are
aware, and in that resided all my blessedness and joy, for
it was the aim and end of all my desires; but ever since
she saw fit to deny me her greeting, my lord Love, in
25 his mercy, has placed all my hope of that same joy in
something which cannot fail me.' At this they began to
talk among themselves, and just as sometimes we see
rain falling mingled with beautiful flakes of snow, so it
seemed to me their words mingled with their sighs.
30 When they had conversed together for a little, she who
had first addressed me said: 'We ask you to tell us in
what this joy of yours resides!' And I, in reply to her,
said this: 'In words which praise my lady.' She an-
swered: 'If you were telling the truth, those words you
35 have composed to describe your state would have been
written in such a way as to convey a different meaning.'
Thinking this over, I moved away feeling almost
ashamed, saying to myself: 'Since there is so much joy
in words which praise my lady, why have I ever written
40 in any other manner?' And so I decided to take as the
theme of my writing from then on whatever was praise
of this most gracious being. Reflecting deeply on this, it
seemed to me that I had undertaken too lofty a theme for
my powers, so much so that I was afraid to enter upon it;
45 and so I remained for several days desiring to write and
afraid to begin.

XIX

1 THEN it happened that as I was walking along a path
beside which flowed a stream of very clear water so

strong an urge to write came over me that I began
to think how I should set about it. I thought it would
not be fitting to speak of my lady to anyone except 5
other women, whom I should address in the second per-
son, and not to any woman but only to those who are
gracious, not merely feminine. Then my tongue spoke,
almost as though moved of its own accord, and said:
'Ladies who know by insight what love is.' With great 10
joy I stored these words away in my mind, intending to
use them as an opening for my rhyme. Then when I had
returned to the city, I pondered for several days and
finally I began a *canzone* which opens with these words,
and is composed in a manner which will appear evident 15
when I come to divide it. The *canzone* begins: *Ladies
who know ...*

> Ladies who know by insight what love is,
>   With you about my Lady I would treat,
>   Not that I think her praises I'll complete,
>   But seeking by my words to ease my mind.
>   When I consider all her qualities
>   I say that Love steals over me so sweet
>   That if my courage then did not retreat
>   By speaking I'd enamour all mankind.
>   Yet words not too exalted I would find,
>   Lest base timidity my mind possess;
>   But lightly touch upon her graciousness,
>   Leaving her worth by this to be divined,
>   With you, ladies and maidens who know love.
> To others it may not be spoken of.
>
> To the all-knowing mind an angel prays:
>   'Lord, in the world a miracle proceeds,
>   In act and visible, from a soul's deeds,

Whose splendour reaches to this very height.'
One imperfection only Heaven has:
The lack of her; so now for her it pleads
And every saint with clamour intercedes.
Only compassion is our advocate.
God understands to whom their prayers relate
And answers them: 'My loved ones, bear in peace
That she, your hope, remain until I please
Where one knows he must lose her, soon or late,
And who will say in Hell: "Souls unconfessed!
I have beheld the hope of Heaven's blessed."'

My lady is desired in highest heaven.
Now of her excellence I'd have you hear.
All ladies who would noble be, draw near
And walk with her, for as she goes her way
A chill in evil hearts by Love is driven,
Causing all thoughts to freeze and perish there.
If any such endured to look on her
He would be changed to good or die straightway.
If any man she find who worthy be
To look at her, her virtue then he knows,
For, greeting him, salvation she bestows,
In meekness melting every grudge away.
With further grace has God endowed her still:
Whoever speaks with her shall not fare ill.

Love says of her: 'How can a mortal thing
Have purity and beauty such as hers?'
Then looks again and to himself he swears
A marvel she must be which God intends.
Pearl-like, not to excess, her colouring,
As suited to a lady's face, appears.
She is the sum of nature's universe.
To her perfection all of beauty tends.

Forth from her eyes, where'er her gaze she bends,
Come spirits flaming with the power of love.
Whoever sees her then, those eyes they prove,
Passing within until the heart each finds.
You will see Love depicted in her face,
There where no man dare linger with his gaze.

My song, you will go parleying, I know,
With many ladies, when I give consent.
Since I have raised you without ornament
As Love's young daughter, hear now what I say.
Of those about you, beg assistance, so:
'Tell me which way to take, for I am sent
To her whose praise is my embellishment.'
If you would journey there without delay
Among the base and vulgar do not stay.
Contrive to show your meaning, if you can,
Only to ladies or a courteous man.
They will conduct you by the quickest way.
You will find Love abiding with her beauty.
Commend me to my Lord, as is your duty.

So that this *canzone* may be well understood, I will
divide it more minutely than the previous verses. First
of all I divide it into three main parts; the first is a pre- 20
lude to the words which follow; the second is the subject
with which I deal; the third is like an attendant on the
words which precede it. The second begins: *To the all-
knowing mind . . .*; and the third: *My song, you will go
parleying. . . .* The first part is subdivided into four sec- 25
tions. In the first I state to whom I wish to speak con-
cerning my lady and why I wish to speak of her; in the
second I describe the condition in which I find myself
when I think of her virtue and what I would say if I did

30 not lose courage; in the third I say how I think I must
speak of her in order not to be hindered by misgivings;
in the fourth, restating to whom I wish to speak, I give
the reason why. The second of these sections begins:
When I consider . . .; the third: *Yet words not too exalted . . .*
35 and the fourth: *With you, ladies . . .*

Next, where I say: *To the all-knowing mind . . .* I begin
to treat of my lady and this part is divided into two sec-
tions. In the first I say what the thoughts of Heaven are
concerning her; in the second I say what is thought of
40 her on earth, beginning: *My lady is desired . . .* This
second section is further subdivided into two; first I
speak of the nobility of her soul and relate some of the
effective powers which emanate from it; secondly I
speak of the nobility of her person, mentioning some of
45 her beauties, beginning; *Love says of her . . .* This second
section is also further subdivided into two, for I speak
first of the beauties of her whole person, and secondly of
the beauty of certain parts of her person, beginning:
Forth from her eyes . . . Here again this subsection is
50 divided into yet another two parts; in the first I speak of
her eyes, which are the beginning of love; in the second
I speak of her mouth, which is the end and aim of love.
And to eliminate here and now all evil thought, let the
reader remember what is written above about my
55 lady's salutation, which was an operation of her mouth,
and was the object of all my desires for as long as it was
granted to me.

Finally, where I say: *My song, you will go parleying . . .*
I add a stanza to serve almost as a handmaiden to the
60 others, in which I say what I desire of my *canzone*. As
this last part is simple to understand I will not involve
myself in further divisions. Certainly to uncover still
more meaning in this *canzone* it would be necessary to

divide it more minutely; but if anyone has not the wit to
understand it with the help of the divisions already made 65
he had best leave it alone. Indeed I am afraid that I may
have conveyed its meaning to too many by dividing it
even as I have done, if it should come to the ears of too
many.

XX

WHEN this *canzone* had circulated among a number of 1
people, a friend who heard it was moved to ask me to
write saying what Love is, having perhaps, because of
the verses he had heard, greater confidence in me than I
deserved. So, reflecting that after the development of my 5
new theme it was appropriate to examine the subject of
Love, and also to please my friend, I decided to write on
this question. Then it was I wrote the sonnet which
begins: *Love and the noble heart* . . .

Love and the noble heart are but one thing,
    Even as the wise man tells us in his rhyme,
    The one without the other venturing
    As well as reason from a reasoning mind.
    Nature, disposed to love, creates Love king,
    Making the heart a dwelling-place for him
    Wherein he lies quiescent, slumbering
    Sometimes a little, now a longer time.
Then beauty in a virtuous woman's face
    Pleases the eyes, striking the heart so deep
    A yearning for the pleasing thing may rise.
    Sometimes so long it lingers in that place
    Love's spirit is awakened from his sleep.
    By a worthy man a woman's moved likewise.

10 This sonnet is divided into two parts. In the first I speak
of Love as he is in potentiality; in the second I speak of
him as potentiality made actual. The second part
begins: *Then beauty* . . . The first part is further divided
into two sections. In the first I say in what subject this
15 potentiality resides; in the second I say how the subject
and potentiality are brought together to produce one
being and I describe how the one is in relation to the
other as form is to matter. The second subsection begins:
Nature, disposed to love . . . Next, where I say *Then*
20 *beauty* . . ., I say how this potentiality is made actual,
first in a man and secondly in a woman, in the line: *By a*
worthy man . . .

XXI

1 WHEN I had discussed the nature of Love in the pre-
ceding rhyme, I felt the desire to compose again; this
time it was to be something in which while praising my
lady I should make plain how Love is awakened through
5 her, and not only awakened where he is sleeping, for
where he is not in potentiality she, by her miraculous
power, causes him to be. So then I wrote this sonnet
which begins: *Love is encompassed* . . .

Love is encompassed in my Lady's eyes
    Whence she ennobles all she looks upon.
    Where e'er she walks, the gaze of everyone
    She draws; in him she greets, such tremors rise,
All pale, he turns his face away, and sighs,
    Reflecting on his failings, one by one.
    Fleeing before her, wrath and pride are gone.
    Come, ladies, sing with me her eulogies,

All gentleness and all humility
　　When she is heard to speak in hearts unfold,
　　And blessed is he by whom she first was seen.
　　When she a little smiles, her aspect then
　　No tongue can tell, no memory can hold,
　　So rare and strange a miracle is she.

This sonnet has three parts. In the first I say how my
lady changes what is potential into act by the most
noble power of her eyes; and in the third I say how she
does the same, by the most noble power of her mouth;
between these two parts is another very short one which
serves as an appeal for assistance in moving from the
preceding to the following; it begins: *Come, ladies, sing...*
and the third part begins: *All gentleness...* The first of
these principal parts is divided into three sections. In the
first I speak of her miraculous power of ennobling
everything she sees, and this amounts to saying that she
calls Love into potentiality where he is not; in the second
I say how she actualizes Love in the hearts of all whom
she sees; in the third I describe the subsequent effects of
her miraculous power over their hearts. The second of
these sections begins: *Where e'er she walks...*; the third:
... in him she greets... Then where I say: *Come, ladies,
sing...* I make it clear to whom I mean to speak, calling
on other women to help me to do her honour. Then,
where I say: *All gentleness...* I repeat what is said in the
first part with reference to two actions of her mouth,
one of which is her sweetest utterance and the other her
smile which stirs such wonder; but what effect her smile
has in people's hearts I do not say because memory can-
not retain it nor its operation.

XXII

1 NOT many days after that, as it pleased the Lord of glory who Himself experienced death, he who had been the father of this wonder which Beatrice was seen to be, departing from our life, passed truly to eternal glory.
5 Such departure is always grievous to friends who are left, and no friendship is so intimate as that between a good father and a good child; and since my lady was of the highest degree of goodness, and her father, as many people believe and as is true, was also a man of great
10 goodness, it is plain that my lady was filled with bitterest sorrow. Since it is the custom in the city I have mentioned for women to foregather with women and men with men on such sad occasions, a number of women met together where Beatrice was weeping piteously.
15 And I, seeing some of them returning, heard them talking about her, saying how she mourned. Among their words I was able to make out the following: 'She weeps so much that truly anyone seeing her must die of compassion.' Then they passed on and I was left in such
20 distress that my face was bathed in tears, and I hid my eyes in my hands again and again. I would have hidden myself away at once as soon as my tears began to flow, but I hoped to hear more about my lady, for where I was most of the women would pass by as they took
25 their leave of her. So I remained in my place and other women passed by, talking about her; and I heard them say: 'How can any of us ever feel happy again after hearing her piteous words?' After them came other women, saying: 'This man here weeps as though he
30 had seen her as we have.' And still others said concerning me: 'Look at this man. You would hardly know him, he

is so changed!' In this way, as these women passed, I heard things about my lady and myself, as I have related. Afterwards, thinking the matter over, I decided, as this was a suitable theme, to put into verse what I had heard 35 these women say. And since I should have liked to question them, if it had not been out of place, I arranged my material as if I had done so and as if they had answered me. I composed two sonnets about it. In the first I ask the questions I wanted to ask; in the other I 40 give the women's reply, based on what I heard them say, as if they had answered me. I began the first sonnet with the words: *You who approach* . . .; and the second: *Are you that person* . . .

> You who approach, in aspect so cast down,
>   And by your lowered gaze your sadness prove,
>   Whence do you come, that all the colour of
>   Your cheeks has turned, it seems, to Pity's own?
> Our gentle lady have you looked upon,
>   Bathing with tears the countenance of Love?
>   Say to me, ladies, what your every move,
>   Ennobled by her, to my heart makes known.
> Coming from sorrow of such gravity,
>   With me, I pray, a little while remain,
>   And what befalls her do not keep from me.
> The marks of weeping in your eyes are plain,
>   And so transfigured you return I see,
>   My heart is shaken even by such pain.

This sonnet is divided into two parts. In the first I 45 address the women and ask them if they come from my lady, telling them that I believe they do since they seem enhanced in graciousness; in the second I entreat them to speak to me of her. The second part begins: *Coming from sorrow* . . . 50

Are you that person who so often spoke
  About our lady, and to us alone?
  Your voice indeed resembles his in tone
  But in your face we find another's look.
  Why do you weep so bitterly that folk
  Are moved as though your sadness were their own?
  Did you our lady weeping come upon
  So that your inward grief you cannot cloak?
Leave us to weep and mournful wend our way,
  (To seek to comfort us would be a sin)
  Recalling what in tears we heard her say.
  So close does Pity to her visage cling
  Whoever in her presence wished to stay
  And gazed at her, had died of sorrowing.

This sonnet has four parts, in accordance with the four
different ways of speaking of the women for whom I
reply; and as they are set out plainly above, I will not
undertake to relate the content of these parts, but
55 merely indicate where the divisions occur. The second
part begins: *Why do you weep* . . .; the third: *Leave us to
weep* . . .; and the fourth: *So close does Pity* . . .

XXIII

1 A FEW days after this, it happened that a painful illness
affected a certain part of my body which caused me
intense pain for nine days on end. This made me so
weak that I lay like someone paralysed. On the ninth
5 day, in the midst of almost unendurable pain, a thought
came to me concerning my lady. And when I had
thought about her for a little while, I fell to thinking
about my own life, now so debilitated, and reflecting

64

how short this life is, even in health, I began to weep
about our wretched state. Sighing deeply, I said to my- 10
self: 'One day, inevitably, even your most gracious
Beatrice must die.' This thought threw me into such a
state of bewilderment that I closed my eyes, and I
began, like a person who is delirious, to be tormented by
these fantasies. First, as my mind began to wander, I 15
saw faces of dishevelled women, who said: 'You too
will die.' And then, after these women, other faces
appeared, strange and horrible to look at, saying: 'You
are dead.' Then, my imagination still wandering, I came
to some place I did not know, where I saw women 20
going about the street, weeping and in disarray, in
terrible distress. I seemed to see the sun grow dark and
stars turn to such a colour that I thought they were
weeping; birds flying in the air fell dead, and the earth
trembled with great violence. As I marvelled in my 25
fantasy, growing very much afraid, I thought that a
friend came to me and said: 'Do you not know? Your
wonderful lady has departed from this world.' Then I
began to weep most piteously, and I wept not only in
my dreams but with my eyes, which were wet with real 30
tears. I thought I was looking up into the heavens, where
I seemed to see a multitude of angels returning to their
realm, and before them floated a little cloud of purest
white. The angels were singing to the glory of God and
the words I seemed to hear were: *Osanna in excelsis*,* and 35
that was all I could make out. Then my heart, which was
so full of love, said to me: 'It is true that our lady is
lying dead.' And when I heard this, I seemed to go to see
the body in which that most noble and blessed soul had
been; and the illusion was so powerful that I saw my 40
lady lying dead, and women seemed to be covering her,

* Hosannah in the highest.

that is, her head, with a white veil. On her face was such
an expression of serenity that she seemed to say: 'I now
behold the fountainhead of peace.' In my dream I was
45 filled with such serenity at the sight of her that I called
on Death and said: 'Sweet Death, come to me; do not
be cruel to me, for you must now have grown gracious
after being in such a presence! Come now to me, for I
greatly desire you; see, I already wear your colour!'
50 When I had seen all the sorrowful necessities completed
which it is customary to perform for the bodies of the
dead, I thought that I returned to my room; there I
looked up towards Heaven and so vivid was my
fantasy that as I wept I began to say in my real voice:
55 'O most beautiful soul, how blessed is he who beholds
you!' As I was sobbing out these words and calling on
Death to come to me, a kind and gentle young woman
who was standing beside my bed, thinking my tears and
cries were caused solely by the pain of my illness, began
60 to weep herself, in great alarm. Whereupon, other
women who were present in the bedroom noticed that
I was weeping by the distress which it was causing her.
Sending away from my bedside this young woman, who
was closely related to me, they drew near to arouse me,
65 thinking I was dreaming, and said: 'Sleep no longer'
and 'Do not be distressed'. And as they spoke, my vivid
dream was broken just at the moment when I was about
to say: 'O Beatrice, blessed are you!' I had already
uttered the words 'O Beatrice' when I opened my eyes
70 with a start and realized I had been dreaming. And
though I did utter her name, my voice was so broken by
my sobs that I had the impression that no one under-
stood. I felt very much abashed, but in response to
Love's prompting, I turned my face towards the women.
75 When they saw me, they began to say: 'He looks as if he

were dead.' And they said to each other: 'Let us see if we
can rally him.' So they said many things to reassure me
and kept asking what had frightened me. When I felt a
little comforted, realizing it had all been a dream, I
answered: 'I will tell you what happened to me,' and so 80
I told them what I had seen from beginning to end,
keeping back only the name of my most gracious lady.
Later, when I had recovered from my illness, I decided
to write some verses about what I had experienced, as it
seemed appropriate as a love-theme. So I wrote this 85
canzone which begins: *A lady, youthful . . .*, the arrange-
ment of which is made clear in the analysis which
follows.

A lady, youthful and compassionate,
    Much graced with qualities of gentleness,
    Who where I called on Death was standing near,
    Beholding in my eyes my grievous state,
    And hearing babbled words of emptiness,
    Began to weep aloud in sudden fear.
    And other women, being made aware
    Of my condition by the one who cried,
    Dismissed her from my side,
    And drew, to rally me, about my bed.
    'Wake from your sleep,' one said;
    And one: 'What has bereft you of all cheer?'
    My strange illusion then I put aside,
    Calling the name of her for whom I sighed.

My voice, by grief made weak, so softly came,
    So broken by the sobs which anguished me,
    Only my heart her name could understand.
    Despite my aspect all imbued with shame,
    Which in my countenance was plain to see

I turned towards them at my Lord's command.
When they then saw me, of all colour drained,
They spoke as if they feared that I was dead.
'Oh, help him in his need!'
Gently they urged each other to the task,
And often they would ask:
'What did you see that left you so unmanned?'
Then when I was a little comforted
'Ladies, to you I'll speak of it,' I said.

'As thinking of my frail life I lay
And how its brief duration is as naught,
Love, dwelling in my heart, began to grieve;
At which my soul was filled with such dismay
That, sighing, I lamented in my thought:
"My lady, too, one day this life must leave."
Such desolation then my mind did cleave
I closed my eyes, lost in despondency.
In their perplexity
My spirits scattered and went wandering.
Then vain imagining,
Far from all truth, such as wild fancies weave,
Showed women's faces looming angrily,
Repeating "Die! You too, you too will die!"'

Then many fearful things my eyes did greet
In the delusive dream which held me fast.
I seemed to be – the place I did not know –
Where women all dishevelled in the street,
Some shedding tears, and others wailing, passed.
Like fiery arrows flew their words of woe.
Across the sun a darkness seemed to grow.
The stars came out and from their heavenly wold
They dropped tears, as of old.
Birds flying in the air fell dead; earth shook;

And with a pallid look
A man appeared and to me whispered low:
"What are you doing? Have you not been told?
Your lovely lady's lying dead and cold."'

'My eyes, with tears suffused, to heaven lifting,
I saw, appearing like a shower of manna,
Angels returning to the realms above.
Ahead of them a little cloud was drifting,
And as they followed it all cried *Hosanna*:
No more they sang than this I tell you of.
Then to reveal the mystery came Love,
Saying to me, "Our lady come and see."
Still in my fantasy,
He brought me where I saw her lying dead,
And gathered round her bed
Women I saw who veiled her in a robe.
With her, in truth, was such humility
She seemed to say, "Peace has been granted me."'

'Sorrow induced in me such humbleness,
When all humility in her I'd seen,
That I could say, "Sweet Death, I'll cherish thee,
For thou art now a thing of graciousness
Since in my lady's bosom thou hast been,
And wilt compassionate, not cruel, be.
So much I long to join thy company
That, see, already death-like I appear
And my heart bids: draw near."
Then I departed, every sad rite done,
And when I was alone,
Looking on high, I said: "Blessèd is he,
Fair soul, who may your goodness gaze upon."
Then at your words I woke, my vision flown.'

This *canzone* has two parts. In the first I relate, address-
90 ing an undefined person, how I was aroused from a delu-
sion by certain women and how I promised to tell them
about it; in the second I give an account of what I told
them. The second part begins: *As thinking of my frail
life*. . . . The first of these parts subdivides into two
95 sections. In the first I say what the women, one of them
in particular, said and did because of my fantasy,
before I had come to myself; in the second I relate what
they said when I had awakened from my delirium; this
section begins: *My voice, by grief made weak*. . . . Then,
100 where I say: *As thinking of my frail life* . . . I relate my
dream as I told it to them, and this part is also sub-
divided into sections. In the first I relate the dream in the
order in which it occurred; in the second, saying at what
moment the women aroused me, I express, indirectly,
105 my gratitude to them. This section begins: *Then at
your words* . . .

XXIV

1 AFTER this delirious dream, it happened one day that as
I was sitting thoughtfully by myself I felt a tremor in my
heart as though I were in my lady's presence. Then a
vision of Love came to me. He seemed to come from the
5 direction where my lady lived, and with great joy he
said to me in my heart: 'Bless now the day I took you in
my power for this you must surely do.' And indeed my
heart seemed so full of joy that I did not know it for my
heart in this unusual state. Soon after these words which
10 my heart spoke to me with the tongue of Love, I saw
approaching me a gracious lady, renowned for her
beauty, who for a long time had been the beloved of my

closest friend. Her name was Giovanna, but some say that because of her beauty she was nicknamed Prima- vera, that is, Spring, and this is what she was usually 15 called. And coming after her, as I looked, I saw the miraculous Beatrice. They passed by quite close to me, one behind the other, and Love seemed to say to me in my heart: 'The first is called Primavera, and the sole reason for this is the way you see her walking today, for 20 I inspired him who gave her this name of Primavera, which means that she will come first (*prima verrà*) on the day Beatrice appears after the dream of the one who serves her faithfully. If you also consider her first name, it too signifies "she will come first", for Joan comes 25 from John, who preceded the True Light, saying *Ego vox clamantis in deserto: parate viam Domini.*'* And afterwards Love seemed also to say these words: 'Anyone who thought carefully about this would call Beatrice Love because of the great resemblance she bears to me!' 30 Thinking about this later, I decided to compose some verses for my best-loved friend, keeping back certain words which it seemed better not to reveal, for I believed that his heart was still in thrall to the beauty of this gracious Primavera; and I wrote this sonnet which 35 begins: *A spirit in my heart . . .*

A spirit in my heart which sleeping lay,
    Being for love created, woke and stirred;
And from afar came Love himself, so gay,
    That scarcely knowing him I thought I erred.
'You must take heed to honour me today,'
    He said, smiling with joy at every word.
While he remained with me, I scanned the way

---

*I am a voice crying in the wilderness: prepare ye the way of the Lord. (cf. *Matthew*, iii, 3.)

In the direction whence had come my Lord,
And saw two whom their friends call Joan and Bee.
Draw near the place where I stood wondering.
One miracle after another came!
Love's words re-echo in my memory:
'She who precedes the other is called Spring,
And she who is my image has my name.'

This sonnet has many parts; in the first I relate how I
felt a familiar tremor in my heart and how Love seemed
suddenly to be there, happy in my heart, having come
40 from far away; the second relates what Love seemed to
say to me in my heart, and how he looked; the third
relates how, when he had been with me a little while, I
saw and heard certain things. The second part begins:
You must take heed . . .; and the third: *While he re-*
45 *mained.* . . . This third part is also divided into two: in
the first section I say what I saw; in the second I say what
I heard. The second section begins: *She who precedes* . . .

XXV

1 AT this point someone whose objections are worthy of
the fullest attention might be mystified by the way I
speak of love as though it were a thing in itself, and not
only a substance endowed with understanding but also a
5 physical substance, which is demonstrably false; for love
is not in itself a substance at all, but an accident in a
substance. That I speak of love as if it were a bodily
thing, and even as if it were a man, appears from these
three instances: I say that I saw him coming; now since
10 'to come' implies locomotion and, according to the
Philosopher, only a body in its own power is capable of

motion from place to place, it follows that I classify love as a body. I say also that he laughed and that he spoke, which things are appropriate to a man, especially the capacity to laugh; and so it follows that I make love 15 out to be a man. To clarify this matter, in a manner that is useful to the present purpose, it should first be understood that in ancient times the theme of love was not taken as a subject for verses in the vernacular but there were authors who wrote on love, namely, certain poets 20 who composed in Latin; this means that among us (and no doubt it happened and still happens in other countries, as in Greece) those who wrote of love were not vernacular but learned poets. It is not very many years ago since the first vernacular poets appeared. I say poets 25 because composing rhymes in the vernacular is not so different from writing verses in Latin, due proportion being borne in mind. That it is not long ago that this happened can be shown to be the case if we study the literature of the *langue d'oc* and of the *lingua del sì*, for 30 there is nothing written in these languages earlier than one hundred and fifty years ago. The reason why a few unpolished writers achieved the reputation of being able to versify is that they were almost the first to write poetry in the *lingua del sì*. The first to write as a verna- 35 cular poet was moved to do so because he wished to make his verses intelligible to a lady who found it difficult to understand Latin. This is an argument against those who compose in rhyme on themes other than love, because this manner of composition was invented from 40 the beginning for the purpose of writing of love. It follows that since greater licence is granted to poets than to writers of prose, and since those who write in rhyme are none other than poets who write in the vernacular, it is reasonable and fitting that greater licence should be 45 granted to them than to others writing in the vernacular; therefore if any figure of speech or rhetorical colour is permitted to Latin poets it is permitted also to those who write in rhyme. Thus if we see the ancient poets spoke 50 of inanimate things as if they had sense and reason, and made them talk to each other, and that they did this not only with real things but also with things which are not real, making things which do not exist speak, and making accidents speak as if they were substances and men, 55 then it is appropriate for someone writing in rhyme to do the same; not, of course, without some justification, but with a reason that can be later made clear in prose. That Latin poets have written in the manner described may be seen by the example of Virgil who says that 60 Juno, a goddess who was hostile to the Trojans, spoke to Aeolus, god of the winds, in the first book of the *Aeneid: Aeole, namque tibi,** and that he replied to her: *Tuus, o Regina, quid optes, explorare labor: mihi jussa capessere fas est.*† In the words of this same poet an in- 65 animate thing speaks to animate things, in the third book of the *Aeneid: Dardanidae duri.*‡ In Lucan an animate thing speaks to an inanimate: *Multum, Roma, tamen, debes civilibus armis;*§ in Horace a man speaks to his own learning, as though to a person; and not only are they 70 words of Horace, but he gives them as a quotation from the good Homer, in his *Poetics: Dic mihi, Musa, virum.*‖

* It was to you, Aeolus, that . . . (*Aeneid*, 1, 65).

† It is for you, my Queen, and for no one else, to decide what you wish to be done; my duty is to carry out your orders (ibid., 1, 76–7).

‡ You rough Trojans (Apollo's oracle is speaking; ibid., III, 94).

§ For all that, Rome, you have profited greatly from the civil wars (*Pharsalia*, 1, 44). Dante was here following a corrupt text. Lucan is addressing Nero, not Rome, and the verb should be *debet*, not *debes*, the meaning being, 'For all that, Rome has profited greatly from the civil wars.'

‖ Tell me, my Muse, about the man . . . (*De Arte Poetica*, 141).

In Ovid, love speaks as though it were a human being, at the beginning of his book entitled *De Remediis Amoris*, where he says: *Bella mihi, video, bella parantur, ait.** This should serve as an explanation to anyone who has 75 doubts concerning any part of this little book of mine. And lest any uneducated person should assume too much, I will add that the Latin poets did not write in this manner without good reason, nor should those who compose in rhyme, if they cannot justify what they say; 80 for it would be a disgrace if someone composing in rhyme introduced a figure of speech or rhetorical ornament, and then on being asked could not divest his words of such covering so as to reveal a true meaning. My most intimate friend and I know quite a number 85 who compose rhymes in this stupid manner.

XXVI

THIS most gracious lady, of whom I have spoken in 1 words preceding the above, found such favour that when she walked down the street people ran to see her; and this filled me with a wonderful happiness. When she was near anyone such reverence possessed his heart 5 that he did not dare to raise his eyes nor to respond to her greeting. Many people, having experienced this, could bear witness to this for me, if anyone did not believe it. Crowned and clothed with humility, she would go her way, displaying no pride at what she saw 10 and heard. Often people said, when she had passed: 'This is no woman; this is one of the fairest angels of Heaven.' And others said: 'She is a miracle; blessed be

---

*'Some fine things, I see, some really fine things are being cooked up here,' said he. (*Remedia Amoris*, I, 2.)

the Lord who can create such marvels!' I say in truth
15 that she appeared so gracious and in every way so pleas-
ing that those who looked at her experienced in them-
selves a sweetness so pure and gentle that they were
unable to describe it; and there was no one who could
look at her without immediately sighing. These and
20 more marvellous things resulted from her influence.
Thinking about this, and wanting to resume the theme
of her praise, I decided to compose something that
would convey the marvellous and beneficent effects of
her power, so that not only those who could see her with
25 their own eyes but others also might know of her what
words are able to convey. I then wrote this sonnet which
begins: *So deeply to be reverenced ...*

So deeply to be reverenced, so fair,
    My lady is when she her smile bestows,
    All sound of speaking falters to a close
And eyes which would behold her do not dare.
Of praises sung of her she is aware,
    Yet clad in sweet humility she goes.
    A thing from Heaven sent, to all she shows
A miracle in which the world may share.
Her beauty entering the beholder's eye
    Brings sweetness to the heart, all sweets above:
    None comprehends who does not know this state;
    And from her lips there seems to emanate
    A gentle spirit, full of tender love,
    Which to the soul enraptured whispers: 'Sigh!'

This sonnet is so simple to understand from what is
related above that it does not require any analysis. There-
30 fore, leaving it, I go on to say that my lady gained such
favour that not only was she honoured and praised, but

because of her many other women also were honoured and praised. When I observed this I wished to draw it to the notice of those who had not seen it, so I decided to compose something else to convey it. I then wrote this 35 other sonnet beginning: *They see all goodness* . . . which tells how her influence affected other women, as will appear from its division.

They see all goodness perfect made who see
My lady among ladies take her place.
Her presence brings them such felicity
They render thanks to God for this sweet grace.
Her beauty has such wondrous quality
It leaves in women's hearts no envious trace;
Clothed in nobility they're seen to be
Who walk with her, and faith and love embrace.
The sight of her is humbling to all things.
Such loveliness is not to her confined,
For honoured her companions are thereby.
To all she does a noble grace she brings.
No one there is who, calling her to mind,
Lost in Love's very sweetness does not sigh.

This sonnet has three parts. In the first I say among whom my lady seemed most wonderful; in the second 40 I say what a gift of grace was her company; in the third I speak of the things she miraculously brought about in others. The second part begins: *Her presence brings* . . .; the third: *Her beauty has.* . . . This last part is subdivided into three sections. In the first I say what she brought 45 about in women, that is, as to themselves; in the second I say what she brought about in them in the eyes of others; in the third I show how not only in women but in everyone, and not only by her presence but in the

50 remembrance of her she had a miraculous influence.
The second section begins: *The sight of her* . . .; and the
third: *To all she does* . . .

XXVII

1 AFTER this I began to reflect one day on what I had
written concerning my lady, that is, in the two pre-
ceding sonnets; and, realizing that I had not spoken of
the effect she was bringing about in me at the present
5 time, I felt that I had expressed myself inadequately. So
I decided to say in rhyme how susceptible I was to her
influence and how her power affected me. As I thought
I could not relate this in the brief span of a sonnet, I
began a *canzone*, of which the first words are: *So long
10 have I been* . . .

> So long have I been subject to Love's sway
>   And grown accustomed to his mastery
>   That where at first his rule seemed harsh to me
> Sweet is his presence in my heart today.
> Thus when all fortitude he takes away,
> So that my frail spirits seem to flee,
> Then I am lost in sweetness utterly
> And pallid looks my fainting soul display.
> Love marshals then against me all his might;
> Routed, my spirits wander, murmuring,
>   And to my lady bring
> Petition for new solace in my plight.
> Thus by her merest glance I am unmanned,
> And pride so humbled, none could understand.

XXVIII

Quomodo sedet sola civitas plena populo! facta est quasi 1
vidua domina gentium.*

I was still composing this *canzone* and had completed
the stanza which I give above when the Lord of justice
called this most gracious lady to partake of glory under 5
the banner of the blessed Queen, the Virgin Mary, whose
name was always uttered in prayers of the utmost
reverence by this blessed Beatrice. Although perhaps it
would be pleasing at this point to discuss her departure
from us, it is not my intention to do so here for three 10
reasons: the first is that to do so does not form part of
the present subject, as can be seen on referring to the
preface which precedes this little book; the second is
that even if it were part of the present subject, no words
of mine would be adequate to treat the subject as it 15
should be treated; the third is that, even supposing that
both the one and the other were not the case, it is not
fitting for me to discuss her death because in so doing I
should be obliged to write in praise of myself, which is
reprehensible above all things. I therefore leave this 20
subject to be discussed by someone else. Nevertheless,
since the number nine has occurred over and over again
in what I have written, and this clearly could not happen
without reason, and since in her departure the number
nine seemed to play an important part, it is appropriate 25
to say something about this as seems relevant to my
theme. Therefore, I will first say what part it played in
her death, and then I shall suggest some reasons why this
number was so closely associated with her.

*How doth the city sit solitary, that was full of people! How is she
become as a widow! (*The Lamentations of Jeremiah*, i, 1–2.)

79

XXIX

1 NOW, according to the Arabian way of reckoning time, her most noble soul departed from us in the ninth hour of the ninth day of the month; according to the Syrian method, she died in the ninth month of the year, 5 because the first month in that system is Tixryn the first, which we call October; and according to our way of reckoning, she departed this life in the year of our Christian era, that is of the years of Our Lord, in which the perfect number had been completed nine times in 10 the century in which she had been placed in this world; for she was born a Christian of the thirteenth century. Why this number was so closely connected with her might be explained as follows. Since, according to Ptolemy and according to Christian truth, there are 15 nine moving heavens, and according to common astrological opinion, these heavens affect the earth below according to their conjunctions, this number was associated with her to show that at her generation all nine of the moving heavens were in perfect conjunction 20 one with the other. This is one reason. But, thinking more deeply and guided by infallible truth, I say that she herself was this number nine; I mean this as an analogy, as I will explain. The number three is the root of nine, because, independent of any other number, multiplied 25 by itself alone, it makes nine, as we see quite plainly when we say three threes are nine; therefore if three is the sole factor of nine, and the sole factor of miracles is three, that is, Father, Son and Holy Ghost, who are three and one, then this lady was accompanied by the number 30 nine to convey that she was a nine, that is, a miracle, of which the root, that is, of the miracle, is nothing other

than the miraculous Trinity itself. Perhaps a more subtle mind could find a still more subtle reason for it; but this is the one which I perceive and which pleases me the most. 35

XXX

AFTER she had departed this life, the city of which I 1 have spoken was left as though widowed, despoiled of all good, and I, still mourning in this city of desolation, wrote to the rulers of the earth, telling them something of its condition, and taking as my beginning the words 5 of the prophet Jeremiah: *Quomodo sedet sola civitas.** I say this so that no one may be surprised that I quote them above, like a heading to the new material that follows. If anyone wished to reproach me because I do not here quote the rest of my epistle, my excuse is that I 10 intended from the beginning to write only in the vernacular, and since the words which follow those I have quoted are all in Latin it would be contrary to my intention if I quoted them all. I am well aware, too, that my closest friend, for whom I write this work, also 15 desired that I should write it entirely in the vernacular.

XXXI

WHEN my eyes had shed tears for so long that they were 1 no longer able to relieve my sorrow, I felt I would like to give vent to it by a sorrowful composition. And so I decided to write a *canzone* in which, in the midst of my lamentation, I would speak of her on whose account 5 grief had so destroyed my soul. And I set to work on a

*How doth the city sit solitary!

81

canzone which begins: *Tears of compassion.* . . . So that this *canzone* may seem the more widowed after its conclusion I will divide it now before I transcribe it, and this method I shall adopt from now on.

I say, then, that this mournful little *canzone* has three parts. The first is the prelude; in the second I speak of my lady; in the third I speak sorrowfully to the *canzone*. The second part begins: *Beatrice has gone* . . .; and the third: *My piteous song.* . . . The first of these three main parts is subdivided into three sections. In the first I say why I am moved to write; in the second I say to whom I wish to address my words; in the third I say of whom I wish to write. The second begins: *And so, as I remember*. . .; and the third: *I'll talk of her.* . . . Then where I say: *Beatrice has gone.* . . . I begin to speak of her; and of this part I make two sections. First I give the reason why she was taken from us; then I say how greatly people mourn her departure; this second section begins: *From the fair person.* . . . This section again divides into three; in the first I say who does not weep for her; in the second I say who does weep; in the third I describe my own state. The second of these sections begins: *But he who seeks* . . .; and the third: *Harsh is the torment.* . . . Finally where I say: *My piteous song* . . . I address the *canzone*, indicating among which ladies it should go and take up its abode.

> Tears of compassion for my grieving heart
> Such torment have inflicted on my eyes
> That, having wept their fill, they can no more.
> Thus, if I still would ease this aching smart,
> Which step by step brings closer my demise,
> Words must bring aid, as weeping did before.
> And so, as I remember how of yore,

While yet my lady lived, I spoke with you,
My gentle ladies, now with you alone,
For I would speak with none
Save those endowed with noble hearts and true,
I'll talk of her with tears, for she is gone.
To Heaven she has suddenly departed,
And here are Love and I left broken-hearted.

Beatrice has gone to Paradise on high
Among the angels in the realm of peace,
And you, ladies, she has left comfortless.
No quality of cold caused her to die,
Nor heat, as brings to others their release,
But only virtue and great gentleness.
For light, ascending from her lowliness,
So pierced the heavens with its radiance,
That God was moved to wonder at the same
And a sweet longing came
To summon to Him such benevolence;
And from on high He called her by her name,
Because our grievous life He saw to be
Unfit for such a noble thing as she.

From the fair person which on earth was hers
Her noble soul departed, full of grace,
To dwell in glory as befits her state.
Whoever speaks of her and sheds no tears,
His heart is stone, so evil and so base,
No living spirit there can penetrate.
He scarcely can her image contemplate
Whose lowly mind and churlish-heartedness
Preclude him from the deepest pangs of grief.
But he who seeks relief
In weeping and would die in his distress,
Of every consolation, like a thief,

Stripping his soul, is one who to his cost
Can clearly bring to mind all we have lost.

Harsh is the torment of each sighing breath
When thoughts recall to my despondent mind
The one for whom my grieving heart is rent;
And often while I'm pondering on Death
The colour leaves my cheeks, so sweet I find
Anticipation of his blandishment.
And sometimes when my thought is fixed intent
Such anguish pierces me on every side,
I start up with the pain by which I'm fraught,
And to such shame I'm brought
That from the company of all I hide.
Then in my solitude, I call, distraught,
On Beatrice, and say: 'Are *you* then dead?'
And while I call on her, I'm comforted.

With tears of sorrow and with tears of anguish
My heart is wearied when I am alone;
Any who heard with pity would be filled;
And what this life has been wherein I languish
Since to the world above my lady's flown,
To tell it all no tongue is there so skilled.
And so, my ladies, even if I willed
I could not truly tell you how I fare,
For by my cruel life of bitter woe
I have been brought so low
That on my deathly pallor all men stare
Seeming to say: 'I leave you to your foe.'
But whatsoe'er I am, my lady sees
And from her mercy still I hope for ease.

My piteous song, now go, and mournfully
Upon those ladies and young maidens wait
To whom I sent, of late,

Your sisters bringing messages of gladness;
And you, who are the daughter of my sadness,
Seek out their company, disconsolate.

XXXII

WHEN this *canzone* had been composed, there came to 1
visit me someone who in the hierarchy of friendship
stands immediately after the first, and he was so closely
related in kinship to my lady now in glory that no one
was closer. After speaking to me a little while he asked 5
me to compose something for a lady who had died,
disguising his words so that it seemed as if he were
talking of someone else who was also dead. Realizing he
was speaking only of our blessed departed one, I said I
would do as he requested. Thinking about the matter 10
afterwards, I decided to write a sonnet in which I would
give some expression to my grief and send it to this
friend of mine, so that it would seem that I had written
it for him. So I wrote the following sonnet, which
begins: *Come, gentle hearts* . . . 15

It has two parts. In the first I call on Love's faithful
followers to hear me; in the second I speak of my
wretched state. The second part begins: *To the relief they
bring* . . .

Come, gentle hearts, have pity on my sighs
  As mournful from my breast you hear them go.
  To the relief they bring my life I owe
Since I should die of sorrow otherwise;
Without them, to make recompense, my eyes,
  More often than I'd wish, alas!, would flow
  To lessen by their tears the weight of woe
Which on my weeping spirit grievous lies.

Many a time you'll hear them calling her,
My gentle lady, who from here was borne
Into a kingdom worthier than this
Of her great virtue; and our life in scorn
Sometimes they will revile, as though they were
The soul itself forsaken by its bliss.

XXXIII

1 WHEN I had written this sonnet, thinking about the
person to whom I intended to give it as though I had
written it for him, I realized that this seemed a poor
and bare service to pay to someone so closely associated
5 with my lady now in glory. So, before giving him the
sonnet, I wrote two stanzas of a *canzone*, one truly for
him and the other for myself, although they both
appear written for the same person to anyone who does
not observe carefully; but anyone who studies them
10 closely sees quite plainly that different people are speak-
ing, since one does not call her his lady, while the other
does, as is evident. Then I gave him the above sonnet
and the following *canzone*, telling him I had written
them all for him. The *canzone* begins: *When I recall.* . . .
15 It has two parts. In one, that is, in the first stanza, this
dear friend of mine and relative of hers makes his
lamentation; in the second stanza it is I who lament,
that is, in the stanza beginning: *Amid my sighing.* . . .
Thus it is plain that in this *canzone* two persons are
20 lamenting, one as a brother, and the other as Love's
servant.

When I recall that nevermore, alas!,
That lady I shall see

On whose account I mourn with such dismay,
My grieving thoughts about my heart amass
Such sorrow that I say:
'My soul, why dost thou not depart from me?
The torments which perforce will burden thee
Here in the world which hateful to thee grows
My mind with fearful apprehension fill.'
To Death then I appeal
As to a sweet, beneficent repose:
'Come now to me,' with so much love I cry
That I am envious of all who die.
Amid my sighing is to be discerned
A sound of plaintiveness
Which calls on Death, lamenting ceaselessly.
To him my every aspiration turned
When in his cruelty
He held my lady fast in his duress.
For then the marvel of her loveliness
To Heaven withdrew and to our sight was lost,
Transformed to spiritual beauty there,
Diffusing everywhere
A light of love which greets the angel-host,
Moving their intellect, so deep and wise,
To wonderment, so full of grace it is.

XXXIV

WHEN the day came that a year was completed since 1
my lady had become a citizen of eternal life, I was
thinking of her as I sat drawing an angel on some
wooden boards. As I worked, I turned my head and saw
standing beside me certain men to whom respect was 5
due. They were watching what I was doing and from

what they later said they had been there some time
before I noticed them. When I saw them I arose and,
greeting them, I said: 'Someone was present in my mind
10 just now and so I was lost in thought.' Then, when they
had gone, I returned to my work of drawing figures of
angels and as I drew, there came to me the idea of
composing some anniversary verses, to be addressed to
those who had just visited me. So then I wrote the
15 sonnet which begins: *Within my mind* ... It has two
beginnings, so I will divide it in two different ways.

The first version of this sonnet has three parts. In the
first I say that my lady was already in my thoughts; in
the second I say how Love influenced me on that
20 account; in the third I speak of the effects of Love. The
second part begins: *Love felt her presence* ...; the third:
Lamenting, from my bosom. ... This second part has two
divisions. In one I say that all my sighs went forth
lamenting; in the second I say that some spoke certain
25 words different from the others. The second section
begins: *But those that issued.* ... Now taking the second
version of the sonnet, it is divided in the same way,
except that in the first part I say at what moment my
lady came into my mind, while in the other I do not say
30 this.

Within my mind there had appeared to me
    The gentle lady whom, by virtue of
    Her perfect goodness, God enthroned above
    In Mary's heaven of humility.

Within my mind there had appeared to me
    The gentle lady who is mourned by Love,
    When you were hither drawn, by virtue of
    Her perfect soul, my handiwork to see.

Love felt her presence in my mind as he
Within my ravaged heart began to move,
And, saying to my sighs, 'Go forth!', he drove
Them hence and they departed dismally.
Lamenting, from my bosom they were rent,
Forming a voice which often and again
Brings to my grieving eyes new tears of woe;
But those that issued with the greatest pain
Murmured 'O noble mind', as forth they went,
'You rose to Heaven this day a year ago.'

XXXV

AFTERWARDS, for some time, because I was in a place
where I remembered days gone by, I became very pen-
sive and filled with such sorrowful thoughts that I took
on an appearance of terrible distress. Becoming aware of
my condition, I raised my eyes to see if anyone noticed
it; and then I saw a gracious lady, young and very
beautiful, who was looking at me from a window so
compassionately, as it seemed from her appearance, that
all pity seemed to be gathered there in her. And so,
because when unhappy people see compassion in others
they are more swiftly moved to weep, as though stirred
to pity for themselves, my eyes began to fill with tears;
then, afraid of revealing the wretchedness of my life,
I withdrew from this lady's gaze. Later I said to myself:
'It must surely be that in that kindest lady's company
there is the most noble love.' Thereupon I decided to
write a sonnet addressed to her and containing what I
have told in this account. As this account is perfectly
clear I will not analyse the sonnet. It begins: *These eyes
of mine . . .*

These eyes of mine beheld the tenderness
    Which marked your features when you turned your
        gaze
    Upon my doleful bearing and the ways
    I many times assume in my distress.
    I understood then that you fain would guess
    The nature of the dolour of my days;
    And so straightway I grew afraid to raise
    My eyes lest they reveal my abjectness.
And as I from your vision then withdrew
    The tears within my heart began to well,
    Where all was stirred to tumult by your sight;
    And to my soul I murmured in my plight:
    'With her indeed that self-same Love must dwell
    Who makes you go thus weeping as you do.'

XXXVI

1 FROM then on wherever this lady saw me her expres-
sion grew compassionate and her face turned pale almost
as though with love, reminding me often of my most
noble lady who was always of a similar colouring.
5 Often indeed when I could not weep or give expression
to my sorrow I used to go to see this compassionate
being, the very sight of whom seemed to draw the tears
from my eyes. And so I felt impelled again to compose
lines addressed to her, and I wrote this sonnet which
10 begins: *No woman's countenance.* . . . Because of the fore-
going account, it has no need of analysis.

    No woman's countenance has ever worn
      In such miraculous degree the hue
      Of love and pity's look, from yielding to
      The sight of gentle eyes or folk who mourn,

As does your own when I approach forlorn
And with my grieving face for mercy sue.
Such thoughts then come to mind because of you
My heart with fear and suffering is torn.
My wasted eyes I find I cannot keep
From gazing at you ever and again,
For by a tearful longing they are led.
Beholding you then so augments their pain
They are consumed by their desire to weep,
Yet in your presence tears they cannot shed.

XXXVII

THE sight of this lady had such an effect on me that my eyes began to delight too much in seeing her, with the result that often I grew angry in my heart and reviled myself greatly. And often too I cursed the vanity of my eyes and said to them in my thoughts: 'Once you moved to tears all who saw you by your sorrowful condition; now it seems that you are ready to forget all that because of this lady who gazes at you; she is not gazing at you at all, except in so far as she is sad about the lady in glory for whom you used to weep. But weep now all you can, for I will remind you of her many times, accursed eyes, for never, this side of death, ought your tears to have ceased!' When I had spoken within myself to my eyes in this way, I was beset with deep sighs of anguish. In order that this battle which was raging within me should not remain locked within the breast of the wretch who was experiencing it, I decided to write a sonnet and include in it a description of this condition which filled me with such horror. And so I wrote the sonnet beginning: *The bitter tears . . .*

It has two parts. In the first I speak to my eyes as my heart spoke within me; in the second I remove a doubt, explaining who it is who speaks in this way. The second part begins: *So speaks my heart.* . . . It could be divided
25 further but this would be superfluous because its meaning is made quite clear by the preceding account.

'The bitter tears which never ceased to flow,
   O eyes of mine, while seasons came and went,
   As you have seen, moved others to lament
   And in their weeping their compassion show;
But now I think you would forgetful grow
   If I, for my part, should prove negligent
   And every cause of this did not prevent,
   Recalling her you mourned not long ago.
Your levity I contemplate with dread
   So that in fear and trembling now I see
   The face of one who holds you with her eyes.
   While life endures you should not ever be
   Inconstant to your lady who is dead.'
So speaks my heart, I hear, and then it sighs.

XXXVIII

1 THE appearance of this lady wrought in me such a strange condition that I often thought of her as of someone who pleased me too much. My thoughts about her were as follows: 'This is a gracious lady, beautiful,
5 young and wise; perhaps she has appeared by Love's will so that my life may know peace.' Often I thought about her more lovingly so that my heart consented to it, that is, to my loving thought. And when I had consented, I reflected, as if moved by reason, and said to

myself: 'Lord, what is this thought that tries to console 10
me in this base fashion and barely lets me think of any-
thing else?' Then another thought rose up and said:
'You have recently been in great tribulation. Why do
you not want to escape from such bitterness? You see
that this is an inspiration of Love, who brings his desires 15
before us, and it proceeds from a most noble source as
are the eyes of the lady who has shown us such compas-
sion.' Having battled within myself in this manner many
times, I decided to compose some more verses on this
subject; and since in the battle of my thoughts those 20
which supported the lady were victorious, it seemed
fitting to address myself to her; so I composed this son-
net, which begins: *Thought which is gentle.* . . . I call it
gentle because it spoke of a gentle lady; in all other
respects it was most base.   25

In this sonnet I divide myself into two parts, according
to the way in which my thoughts were divided. One
part I call my heart, that is desire; the other I call my
soul, that is reason; and I relate what they say to each
other. That it is appropriate to call desire the heart, and 30
reason the soul is quite plain to those to whom I wish the
matter to be clear. It is true that in the preceding sonnet
I take the part of the heart against that of the eyes, and
that seems contrary to what I say in the present one.
Therefore I say that there also I mean the heart to signify 35
desire because my desire to remember my most gracious
lady was still greater than to see the new one, although I
already had some desire to do so, but it seemed slight.
From this it is plain that the one interpretation is not
contrary to the other.   40

This sonnet has three parts. In the first I begin to tell
this lady how my desire turns wholly towards her; in
the second I relate how my soul, that is reason, speaks to

the heart, that is desire; in the third I give the heart's
45 reply. The second begins: *The soul then* . . .; the third
begins: *The heart replies* . . .

Thought which is gentle, since it speaks of you,
    Comes frequently to dwell with me a while.
    Of love it reasons in so sweet a style
    The heart is vanquished and consents thereto.
    The soul then of the heart inquires, 'Pray, who
    Is this who would our intellect beguile?
    And is his virtue such as to exile
    All other contemplation from our view?'
The heart replies: 'O meditative soul,
    This little spirit, newly sent by Love,
    Its longings and desires before me brings.
    Its life and power are emanations of
    The glances of the Lady Pitiful
    Who felt compassion for our sufferings.'

XXXIX

1 IN opposition to this opponent of reason there rose up
one day within me, almost at the ninth hour, a vivid
impression in which I seemed to see Beatrice in glory,
clothed in the crimson garments in which she first
5 appeared before my eyes; and she seemed as young
as when I first saw her. Then I began to think about her
and as I recalled her through the sequence of time past
my heart began to repent sorrowfully of the desire by
which it had so basely allowed itself to be possessed for
10 some days against the constancy of reason; and when this
evil desire had been expelled all my thoughts returned

once more to their most gracious Beatrice. And I say
that from then onwards I began to think of her so much
with the whole of my remorseful heart that frequently
my sighs made this evident, expressing as they issued 15
what my heart was saying, that is, the name of this most
gracious soul and how she had departed from us. It
often happened that a thought would be so laden with
grief that I forgot what the thought had been and where
I was. As a result of the rekindling of my sighs, my weep- 20
ing which had abated was also refuelled to such an extent
that my eyes were like two objects desirous only of
shedding tears; and it often happened, because I wept
for so long, that my eyes were ringed with dark red,
which happens as a result of some illnesses which people 25
suffer. Thus it seems that they were justly rewarded for
their inconstancy, so much so that from then onwards I
could not look at anyone who might return my gaze in
such a way as to cause my eyes to weep again. Then, as I
wanted this evil desire and vain temptation to be shown 30
to be destroyed, so that the verses I had written pre-
viously should raise no doubts in anyone, I decided to
write a sonnet to convey the substance of this narration.
So I then wrote: *Alas! by the violence of many sighs*. I
said 'Alas' because I was ashamed that my eyes had 35
indulged in such inconstancy.

I will not divide this sonnet because the foregoing
account of it makes it quite clear.

> Alas! by the violence of many sighs
>   Born of the thoughts I harbour in my breast,
>   I cannot meet the gaze of others, lest
>   I bring new torment to my vanquished eyes:
>   Two orbs of longing now, their solace is
>   To flow with tears and only grief attest.

So much they weep that Love makes manifest
An encircling crown which suffering implies.
These thoughts of mine and sighs which forth I send
Within my heart to sharper anguish grow,
Where Love in mortal pallor lies in pain;
For in the deep recesses of their woe
The sweet name of my Lady they have penned
And many words to tell her death again.

XL

1 AFTER this tribulation it happened, at the time when
many people go on pilgrimages to see the blessed image
which Jesus Christ has left us as an imprint of His most
beautiful countenance, which my lady in glory now sees,
5 that some pilgrims were passing along a road which runs
almost through the centre of the city where that most
gracious lady was born, lived and died. These pilgrims,
it seemed to me, were very pensive as they went their
way; and so, thinking about them, I said to myself:
10 'These people seem to be journeying from far away,
and I do not think they have ever even heard of my
lady; they know nothing about her, indeed their
thoughts are on quite other things than those that are
around them here; perhaps they are thinking of their
15 friends at home, of whom we know nothing.' Then I
said to myself: 'I know that if they came from a nearby
town they would look distressed as they passed through
this sorrowing city.' Then I said: 'If I could detain them
for a little while, I would surely make them weep
20 before they left, for I would say things which would
reduce to tears everyone who heard me.' And so, when
they had passed from my sight, I decided to write a

sonnet in which I would set forth what I said to myself; and to make it more moving, I decided to write it as if I had spoken to them. So I wrote the sonnet which 25 begins: O *pilgrims*. ... I called them pilgrims in the general sense of the word; for 'pilgrim' may be understood in two ways, one general and one particular, in as much as anyone journeying from his own country is a pilgrim. In the particular sense, pilgrim means someone 30 who journeys to the sanctuary of St James and back. It should be understood that those who travel in the service of the Almighty are of three kinds. Those who travel overseas are called palmers, as they often bring back palms; those who go to St James's shrine in Galicia are 35 called pilgrims, because the burial place of St James was further away from his country than that of any other apostle; and romeos are those who go to Rome, which is where those whom I call pilgrims were going.

I do not divide this sonnet since it is quite clear from 40 the foregoing account.

> O pilgrims, meditating as you go,
>   On matters, it may be, not near at hand,
>   Have you then journeyed from so far a land,
>   As from your aspect one may plainly know,
>   That in the sorrowing city's midst you show
>   No sign of grief, but onward tearless wend,
>   Like people who, it seems, can understand
>   No part of all its grievous weight of woe?
> If you will stay to hear the tale unfold
>   My sighing heart does truly promise this:
>   That you will go forth weeping when I've done.
>   This city's lost her source of blessedness,
>   And even words which may of her be told
>   Have power to move tears in everyone.

XLI

1 LATER two gracious ladies sent word to me, requesting me to send them certain of my verses. Reflecting on their noble lineage, I decided to send them a new composition, written specially for them, together with
5 those they had asked for, in order that I might fulfil their request the more worthily. So I then wrote a sonnet describing my state and sent it to them with the previous sonnet and with another which begins: *Come, gentle hearts* . . .

10 The sonnet which I wrote specially for them begins: *Beyond the widest* . . . It is divided into five parts. In the first I say where my thought goes, and I call it a sigh, naming it thus after one of its effects; in the second I say why it ascends where it does, that is, what causes it to
15 ascend; in the third I say what it sees, that is a lady in glory; and then I call it a pilgrim spirit, for spiritually it ascends into the heavens, and there abides for a while, like a pilgrim who is away from his own country; in the fourth I say that it sees her so beatified, that is, possessed
20 of such attributes, that I cannot comprehend, that is to say, my thought ascends so far into the quality of her being that my intellect cannot follow it; for our intellect in the presence of those blessed souls is as weak as our eyes before the sun; and this is confirmed by the Philo-
25 sopher in the second book of his *Metaphysics*; in the fifth part I say that although I cannot comprehend the place to which my thought takes me, that is, into the presence of her miraculous nature, I understand this at least, that this thought of mine is entirely concerned with my lady,
30 for frequently I hear her name. At the end of this fifth part I say: 'Beloved ladies', to convey that it is to ladies

to whom I write these lines. The second part begins: *A new celestial*; the third: *As it nears* ...; the fourth: *Gazing at her* ...; and the fifth: *That noble one* ...

Beyond the widest of the circling spheres *impirium*
A sigh which leaves my heart aspires to move.
Pilgrim Spirit
A new celestial influence which Love
Bestows on it by virtue of his tears
Impels it ever upwards. As it nears
Its goal of longing in the realms above
The pilgrim spirit sees a vision of
A soul in glory whom the host reveres.
Gazing at her, it speaks of what it sees
In subtle words I do not comprehend
Within my heart forlorn which bids it tell.
That noble one is named, I apprehend,
For frequently it mentions Beatrice;
This much, beloved ladies, I know well.

XLII

AFTER this sonnet there appeared to me a marvellous 1
vision in which I saw things which made me decide to
write no more of this blessed one until I could do so
more worthily. And to this end I apply myself as much
as I can, as she indeed knows. Thus, if it shall please Him 5
by whom all things live that my life continue for a few
years, I hope to compose concerning her what has
never been written in rhyme of any woman. And then
may it please Him who is the Lord of courtesy that my
soul may go to see the glory of my lady, that is of the 10
blessed Beatrice, who now in glory beholds the face of
Him *qui est per omnia secula benedictus.* *

* Who is blessed for ever.

NOTE ON THE STRUCTURE
OF THE VITA NUOVA

The thirty-one poems of the *Vita Nuova* are arranged in the following structural design:

> 10 short poems, 1 long *canzone*, 4 short poems,
> 1 long *canzone*, 4 short poems, 1 long *canzone*,
> 10 short poems.

The mid-point of this pattern is the second long *canzone*. With its 'supporting' eight short poems, four preceding and four following, it is the centre of a central group of nine, the number with which Beatrice is associated, and of which the root is three, the symbol of the Trinity. The central nine is flanked by two integers, which are flanked by two tens (the perfect number), thus:

$$10 + 1 + 9 + 1 + 10$$

Dante does not draw attention to this numerical symmetry, nor is it in any way intrusive. Nevertheless it is present and it shows the importance which Dante attached not only to the significance of numbers but also to the architectural composition of his work. This is a feature which is especially characteristic of the *Divina Commedia*.

NOTES ON THE TEXT

1, 3: *Incipit vita nova*: the last two words of this Latin phrase
have given rise to the Italian title of this work, *La Vita Nuova*.
Their precise meaning is uncertain. In classical Latin *novus*
meant not only 'new' but also 'first', 'inexperienced', 'un-
tried'; it could also mean 'wonderful', 'marvellous', 'unheard
of'. The Italian phrase *vita nuova* does not occur in the present
text except in the title, but it is used in a passage in the *Purga-
torio* in which Beatrice, speaking to the angels concerning
Dante, says:

> *Questi fu tal nella sua vita nova,*
> *Virtualmente, ch'ogni abito destro*
> *Fatto averebbe in lui mirabil prova.*

> This man was such in his new life,
> Potentially, that every good endowment
> Might have shown a wondrous result in him.
>
> (Canto XXX, 115–17)

In the context the phrase seems to mean 'youth' but some
commentators have seen in it a reference to the present work
and consider that it means the new life which began for him
when he first saw Beatrice.

The basic meaning of this Latin rubric is probably 'youth'
or 'early life'. It is unlikely that Dante intended it to stand as a
heading for the entire work; in fact, there are indications that
it is only the first of several headings. He refers to other pos-
sible ones at the end of chapter II, and chapter XXVIII opens with
a quotation in Latin from the *Lamentations of Jeremiah*, which
Dante justifies in chapter XXX as standing 'like a heading to the
new material that follows'.

The words *Incipit vita nova* probably refer only to chapters I
and II, and may be appropriately translated 'Here begins the
period of my boyhood'. The title, *La Vita Nuova*, has acquired

by tradition a more comprehensive meaning, covering the span of life represented in the whole work, that is from the age of nine to about thirty. The literal English translation, 'The New Life', has religious overtones which are probably not in the original.

II, 1: *the heaven of the light*: i.e. the heaven of the sun. According to pre-Copernican astronomy, the earth was the centre of the universe. Around it circled seven planets, of which the sun was the fourth. In separate concentric heavens, they were carried round the earth once every twenty-four hours. As well as this diurnal movement, each heaven had an individual movement of its own. The sun, for instance, while revolving with the other six planets from east to west once every day and night, also revolved slowly from west to east, taking a solar year to complete this independent motion. By saying that the heaven of the sun had almost completed nine of its own circles since his birth, Dante indicates that he was almost nine years old when he first saw Beatrice (traditionally, in May 1274).

II, 5: *She was called Beatrice by many who did not know what it meant to call her this*: it is Boccaccio who first tells us that the Beatrice of the *Vita Nuova* and of the *Divina Commedia* was Beatrice dei Portinari of Florence, who married Simone dei Bardi and died in 1290. Dante's reference to her name in this passage is so ambiguous that some commentators consider that he means to convey that she was an abstract beneficent influence personified as a woman with the symbolic name of Beatrice ('she who blesses'). His words are here interpreted to mean that her name, Beatrice, suited her better than many knew who called her by it.

II, 7: *the heaven of the fixed stars*: beyond the seven heavens containing the planets was an eighth heaven which carried the constellations. These were called 'fixed stars' because in comparison with the planets they appeared to have no independent motion. But the eighth heaven also, as well as revolving with the others once every twenty-four hours round the earth, very slowly traced a course from west to east, taking 100 years to complete one degree, or 36,000 years to complete one circle. By saying that the heaven of the fixed stars had moved one-twelfth of a degree to the east since the birth of Beatrice, Dante indicates that she was eight years and four months old.

II, 15: *the vital spirit*: Dante follows Hugh of St Victor in identi-fying three principal forces of life in the body, which he calls spirits. The 'vital spirit' is the force which is centred in the heart. The 'spirit of the senses' is centred in the brain. The 'natural spirit' is centred in the liver. In addition to these three main forces, there are the senses, which Dante also personifies as spirits, attributing emotion and dialogue to them. (See chapter XI.)

II, 21: *the place to which all our sense perceptions are carried*: i.e. the brain.

II, 25: *where our nourishment is digested*: i.e. the liver.

II, 36: *the words of the poet Homer*: in the *Iliad*, Book XXIV, line 258, Priam says, speaking of Hector: 'He did not seem the son of mortal man, but of a god.' Dante, who knew no Greek, had read this in a Latin translation of Aristotle's *Ethics*, Book VII, chapter 1. He refers to this passage again in two later works, *Il Convivio* ('The Banquet') and *Monarchia* ('Monarchy'); in these instances it appears that Dante understands Aristotle to use this quotation from Homer in support of the belief that some human beings are so noble as to justify their being called divine. Of these, Beatrice is one.

II, 45: *omitting many things which might be copied from the master-text*: the 'master-text' is the 'book' of Dante's memory. It is not his intention to copy everything from it, nor even every-thing that comes under the first heading.

III, 1: *exactly nine years*: According to tradition, the meeting referred to here occurred in May 1283. Dante had often seen Beatrice in the interval (cf. chapter II) but this meeting, nine years after the first, appears to have had the quality of a revelation.

III, 2: *this gracious being*: The Italian word *gentile* has no adequate equivalent in English. 'Gentle' implies too little, and too much that is irrelevant. 'Gracious' will sometimes, but not always, serve. Similarly the word *donna* can sometimes be translated as 'lady', but in other contexts 'woman', 'being', or 'person' seems more appropriate. Some measure of the exaltation of Dante's style must be conveyed, but modern English prose, if heightened too much, is in danger of toppling into bathos. On the other hand, to suggest that all the *donne* of the *Vita Nuova* were 'girls, just girls' is to go from the sublime to the ridiculous.★ A process of consecration is evident throughout the work.

III, 12: *the ninth hour of the day*: According to medieval reckoning, there were twelve day hours and twelve night hours; the day hours were those between sunrise and sunset, the night hours were those between sunset and sunrise. Twice a year, at the spring and autumn equinox, the hours of the day and the hours of the night were equal in length. With the advance of summer, the daylight hours increased in length, though still remaining twelve in number. After the summer solstice (21 June), the daylight hours became shorter and those of the night longer. Sunrise was reckoned as beginning at 6 a.m., the first hour of the day. At the spring equinox (21 March) the ninth hour of the day was 3 p.m. by our reckoning; in May it was nearer 4 p.m.

III, 13: *the first time she had ever spoken to me*: Dante must have heard her voice before, but it appears from this that she had not previously addressed him directly.

★ E. R. Vincent: 'The Crisis in the Vita Nuova', *Centenary Essays on Dante*, Oxford University Press, 1965, p. 135.

III, 20: *a lordly figure*: this is love personified.

III, 41: *a number of poets who were famous at that time*: Among the established poets who wrote in the vernacular were Guittone of Arezzo, Chiaro Davanzati, Bonagiunta of Lucca, Cino of Pistoia, Terino of Castelfiorentino, Dante of Maiano and Guido Cavalcanti.

III, 42: *as I had already tried my hand at the art of composing in rhyme*: Among Dante's early poems are five sonnets on the subject of love addressed to his namesake, Dante of Maiano. These were probably written when Dante was about seventeen years old.

III, 51: *replies from many*: Only three replies have been preserved, one from Dante of Maiano, one from Cino of Pistoia (or from Terino of Castelfiorentino) and one from Guido Cavalcanti.

III, 55: *my closest friend*: i.e. Guido Cavalcanti.

III, 57: *he learned that it was I who had sent him the sonnet*: It was the custom for young poets to send poems anonymously to others who were already established.

III, 59: *The true meaning . . . is perfectly clear*: Dante here interprets the dream as a prophecy of the death of Beatrice. It is not known what interpretation he intended when he wrote the poem.

IV, 1: *my natural spirit*: See Note to chapter II, 15–25.

V, 2: *in a place where words about the Queen of glory were heard*: i.e. in a church, where hymns were being sung in praise of the Virgin.

V, 21: *a few little things for her in rhyme*: Among Dante's early love poems, addressed to other women than Beatrice, are several graceful and charming trifles, probably intended to be set to music.

v, 24: *apart from one*: This is the double sonnet beginning *O you who on the road of love pass by.*

vi, 6: *an epistle in the form of a 'serventese'*: This has not been preserved. In Provençal literature a *serventese* was originally a homage poem, addressed to a feudal lord. It later came to be an exhortatory poem of praise or blame. In Italian, the form of the *serventese* was used for love poetry.

vii, 12: *O you who on the road of Love pass by*: This is a double sonnet, a form said to have been invented by Guittone of Arezzo. Only three double sonnets by Dante are known to us, two of which are contained in the *Vita Nuova*, this and the one beginning, *Death villainous and cruel.*

vii, 20: *beginning and end of the sonnet*: i.e. the first six and the last eight lines.

viii, 10: *I touched on this in the last part*: i.e. in the last two lines of the sonnet beginning *Death villainous and cruel.*

viii, 28: *a person left undefined, although defined in my own intention*: i.e. perhaps himself.

ix, 3: *travel in the direction of the region . . .*: Where was Dante travelling? It has been suggested that he refers here to an expedition of the Florentine militia, which took part in the attack on Castel di Poggio di Santa Cecilia where a rebellion against the Guelf League had been instigated by the Ghibellines of Arezzo. This enterprise, begun in October 1285, lasted until April of the following year, when the castle surrendered.

ix, 10: *my source of happiness*: i.e. Beatrice.

IX, 15: *a beautiful stream of clearest water*: i.e. the Arno, at which Love gazes as though longing to follow its course to Florence.

X, 12: *... departing somewhat from the immediate subject ...*: Dante's subject is his poetry and the events and feelings which inspired it. The following description of the effect on him of the greeting of Beatrice is 'somewhat' of a digression.

XI, 9: *a spirit of love ... spirits of vision ...*: Dante here personifies his feeling and senses as though they were separate parts of his being. (See also Note to chapter II, 15–25.)

XII, 8: *The Lady of courtesy*: Probably the Virgin Mary, but some commentators think that Beatrice is intended. The word *cortesia* is used by Dante elsewhere to mean compassion, or grace. In chapter XLII, 9 God is called the 'Lord of courtesy'.

XII, 16: *Fili mi ... simulacra nostra*: The 'false images' are presumably the screen ladies to whom Dante has shown love in order to keep secret his love for Beatrice.

XII, 23: *Ego tanquam ... autem non sic*: Love seems here to be distinguishing between the general and the particular. Love in general is related to the whole of life and equally to all mankind. Love therefore weeps at the thought that Dante must now withdraw his love from the second screen-lady. In realistic terms, Dante feels a pang of regret on realizing that, though love is universal, he, an individual, cannot love diffusely, but must love one and one only. He has reached the moment of choice, which for finite minds involves exclusion.

XII, 28: *Do not ask more than is useful for you*: These words echo St Paul who in Romans xii, 3 bids us 'not to know more than it is meet to know, but to know in due measure'. Dante quotes them in *Convivio* IV, 13.

XII, 54: *the ninth hour of the day*: See Note to chapter III, 12.

XII, 68: *I intend to clarify and resolve this doubt later on in this little book*: Dante takes up the question of personification in poetry in chapter XXV.

XIII, 17: *Nomina sunt consequentia rerum*: The origin of this sentence is unknown.

XIV, 4: *a friend*: It is not known who this friend was. According to laws governing weddings and funerals in Florence of Dante's time, each invited guest was entitled to bring a companion with him. A knight was entitled to bring four companions, a judge or a doctor, three. Dante seems to have been the companion chosen by a guest who was not a knight, a judge or a doctor, but that is all we can deduce concerning him.

XIV, 5: *so many beautiful women*: not more than twenty-five, including the bride, according to the same laws.

XIV, 7: *his friend*: i.e. Dante.

XIV, 14: *when she sat down at table*: The courses at weddings were limited to three, not counting fruit and sugared almonds.

XIV, 25: *Then my spirits . . .*: See Note to chapter II, 15–25.

XIV, 45: *I had set foot . . . returning*: i.e. he had been brought to the verge of death.

XV, 1: *After this strange transformation*: i.e. the experience he has undergone in the presence of Beatrice at the wedding.

XVII, 1: *these three sonnets*: Sonnets 7, 8 and 9 in which Dante describes the effect on him of the sight and thought of Beatrice.

XVII, 3: *I thought it right to be silent and say no more*: In the three sonnets to which he refers Dante considers he has said everything possible concerning the state of his mind and heart in relation to Beatrice. What he will write henceforth will be praise of her.

XIX, 2: *a stream of very clear water*: Commentators are divided in their views as to whether this is the stream mentioned in chapter IX. If so, it is the Arno. If not, it may be one of the many streams which watered the countryside near Florence.

XIX, *Canzone*, Stanza 2, 12: *Where one knows he must lose her . . . Heaven's blessed*: Dante is here probably referring to the possibility of his own damnation. There seems to be no valid reason for believing that the words 'and who will say in Hell' imply that Dante had already envisaged writing the *Inferno* at the time of the composition of this *canzone*. Similar allusions to Hell and to the poet's damnation, consoled by the memory of the beloved, are to be found in love poetry of the period and immediately preceding.

The contradiction between these lines and those concluding the third stanza, ('With further grace has God endowed her still, Whoever speaks with her shall not fare ill') may perhaps be resolved by reading into the word 'speaks' ('*chi l'ha parlato*' in the original, 'whoever has spoken with her'), a meaning of harmonious relationship, from which at the time of writing this *canzone* Dante feels himself excluded.

XIX, 43: *effective powers*: i.e. results of her nobility of soul.

XIX, 68: *if it should come to the ears of too many*: Dante did not intend to reveal the meaning of this poem to all and sundry. Compare the last two lines of the poem itself.

XX, 1: *When this canzone had circulated*: It was fairly well known by 1292.

XX, 2: *a friend*: Possibly Guido Cavalcanti, though he is usually referred to by Dante as his 'most intimate friend'.

xx Sonnet, Stanza 1, 2: *the wise man*: This epithet (*saggio*, in Italian) was commonly applied to poets in Dante's time. The poet referred to here is Guido Guinizelli.

xxii, 3: *the father of this wonder*: If, as is generally believed, Beatrice is to be identified with Beatrice dei Portinari, her father was Folco di Ricovero di Folco dei Portinari, who lived not far from Dante's family. He was a prominent citizen of Florence, holding governmental office and being elected Prior in August 1282. In 1288 he founded the hospital of Santa Maria Nova. He died on 31 December 1289. From his will, dated 15 January 1288, it appears that Beatrice was by this time married to Simone dei Bardi.

xxiii, 1: *A few days after this*: i.e. a few days after the funeral. It is not known what Dante's illness was. It occurred evidently in the winter of 1290, Dante being then twenty-five. As a few days previously he had been out in the winter weather, weeping as he saw the mourners returning from the house of the Portinari, he may have succumbed to pleurisy or pneumonia. He seems, from the poem, to have had a high temperature and to have been in delirium.

xxiii, 63: *this young woman, who was closely related to me*: She is believed to be one of Dante's two step-sisters, born of his father's second marriage to Lapa di Chiarissimo Cialuffi. One, named Tana, married Lapo di Riccomanno Pannocchia. The other, whose Christian name is not known, married Leone di Poggio and had a son, Andrea, whom Boccaccio described as bearing a physical resemblance to Dante, from which we may deduce that Dante resembled his father more closely than his mother.

xxiii, 90: *addressing an undefined person*: i.e. in contrast to the first *canzone*, which is addressed to 'Ladies who know by insight what love is'.

XXIV, 11: *a gracious lady renowned for her beauty*: This is Giovanna, the lady loved by Guido Cavalcanti.

XXIV, 18: *one behind the other*: In the narrow streets of Florence, with their even narrower footpaths, it is often impossible to walk two abreast.

XXIV, 21: *I inspired him who gave her this name*: i.e. Guido Cavalcanti, who gives Giovanna the name of Primavera in his poem, beginning *Fresca rosa novella, piacente Primavera* (O fresh, new rose, O pleasing Spring).

XXIV, 33: *for I believed his heart was still in thrall*: Dante implies that Cavalcanti, at the time of the composition of the poem, would not have been pleased to hear Love's words concerning the symbolic relationship of Giovanna to Beatrice.

XXIV, Sonnet, Stanza II, 1: *Joan and Bee*: These are English equivalents of the Italian abbreviations *Vanna* and *Bice*, used by Dante in the poem. It is said that Beatrice dei Portinari was called Bice.

XXV, 4: *not only a substance endowed with understanding but also a physical substance*: In scholastic theology, a *substance* is a thing existing in itself; an *accident* resides in a *substance*, being, as we should now say, the *property* of a thing existing in itself. Thus grass is a substance, and greenness is an accident of that substance, it being the property of grass to be green. Love is not a substance but the property of substances (e.g. men capable of loving). Dante, personifying love, is treating an accident as a substance.

XXV, 11: *the Philosopher*: i.e. Aristotle.

XXV, 32: *one hundred and fifty years ago*: The *Vita Nuova* is believed to have been written in the 1290s. This would mean that Dante knew of no literature in the *langue d'oc* (Provençal) or in Italian earlier than 1140. This is valid for Italian but not for Provençal.

xxv, 33: *a few unpolished writers*: This may be an allusion to Giacomo of Lentino, Orbiciani of Lucca and Guittone of Arezzo.

xxv, 35: *the first to write*: Dante here leaves out of account earlier didactic and moralizing verse in Provençal and Italian.

xxv, 40: *this manner of composition*: i.e. writing rhymed verse in Italian.

xxv, 46: *others writing in the vernacular*: i.e. prose writers.

xxv, 76: *concerning any part of this little book*: Dante is referring to chapter XII in which he has promised to explain his reasons for the use of personification in his verses.

xxv, 85: *My most intimate friend*: i.e. Guido Cavalcanti, who has evidently discussed poetry with Dante at some length.

xxvi, 21: *wanting to resume the theme of her praise*: This theme had been interrupted by the death of Beatrice's father, on the occasion of which Dante had written the two sonnets included here, and by his illness, which inspired the second *canzone*. These poems, though they are inspired by Beatrice, are not specifically concerned with praise of her. The sonnet beginning 'A spirit in my heart' concerns an exalted vision of Beatrice in relation to Giovanna, but it appears that Dante does not regard it as belonging to those poems in which he treats of the 'new and nobler theme' announced in chapter XVII.

xxviii, 1: *Quomodo sedet . . . gentium*: These are the first words of the Lamentations of Jeremiah. In chapter XXX Dante justifies their introduction here as standing 'like a heading to the new material that follows'. Like Jerusalem, Florence has tried the patience of God, who has withdrawn Beatrice from earth to Heaven.

XXVIII, 6: *under the banner of* . . .: i.e. in the company of souls who are near the Virgin. When Dante beholds Beatrice in glory in *Paradiso* he finds that she is seated in the third circle of the Heavenly Rose, beside Rachel, who sits below Eve, who sits below the Virgin.

XXVIII, 12: *the present subject*: i.e. the presentation and exposition of his poems.

XXVIII, 13: *the preface which precedes this little book*: Dante is, it may be supposed, referring to chapter 1 in which he has said that he intends to copy the words contained in the book of his memory, 'or if not all, at least their meaning'. It has been suggested, however, that there was another preface in which the scope and intention of the work was more explicitly set forth, and which has not come down to us.

XXVIII, 15: *no words of mine* . . . *as it should be treated*: The death of Beatrice was, it seems, envisaged as a theme so exalted that it would have been beyond Dante's poetic powers. He does, however, proceed (in chapters XXIX and XXXI and in the *canzone* beginning 'Tears of compassion') to speak of her death and of its effect upon him. What he here declines to say must relate to aspects of the role of Beatrice for which he did not feel adequately prepared (cf. chapter XLII).

XXVIII, 19: *in so doing I should be obliged to write in praise of myself*: Dante perhaps means that in discussing the meaning, for him, of Beatrice's death (and life) he would have to reveal what he believed to be her role towards him as an intercessor with God.

XXVIII, 21: *someone else*: Perhaps Cino of Pistoia, who wrote a *canzone* on the death of Beatrice, in which he represents her as communing with the blessed concerning Dante.

XXVIII, 22: *the number nine ... in what I have written*: i.e. in chapters II, III, VI, XII and XXIII.

XXIX, 1: *according to the Arabian way of reckoning time*: Dante's knowledge of this was derived from the *Elementa astronomica* by Alfraganus.

XXIX, 3: *the ninth day of the month*: i.e. according to the Arabian reckoning, corresponding, in the month in question (June), to the 19th day, in our reckoning.

XXIX, 3: *according to the Syrian method*: See below.

XXIX, 4: *the ninth month of the year*: i.e. June, which is the sixth month according to the Roman reckoning. See below.

XXIX, 5: *the first month in that system is Tixryn the first, which we call October*: The following comparative table makes this passage clear:

Syrian method		Roman method	
1. Tixryn the first	corresponding to	October	(10)
2. Tixryn the second		November	(11)
3. Canon the first		December	(12)
4. Canon the second		January	(1)
5. Xubât		February	(2)
6. Adâr		March	(3)
7. Nisân		April	(4)
8. Eijâr		May	(5)
9. Hazirân		June	(6)
10. Tamûz		July	(7)
11. Ab		August	(8)
12. Eilûl		September	(9)

XXIX, 9: *the perfect number ... in this world*: The 'perfect' (or complete) number is 10. It had been completed nine times in the century in which Beatrice was born, i.e. she died in 1290, and on 19 June. (See above.) The year 1290 corresponds in Arabian reckoning to the year 689, which, according to our reckoning began on 14 January. The Arabian Giumâda, which corresponds to our June and July, began on 11 June. The ninth day of Giumâda was therefore the nineteenth of our June.

Dante has recourse to three calendars to identify the date of the death of Beatrice. This miraculously coincided in all three reckonings with the number 9 and also with the perfect number 10 in our reckoning.

XXIX, 14: *Ptolemy*: i.e. the astronomer. Dante had no direct knowledge of his works. He knew Alfraganus' compendium of them, *Almagest*. It is Aristotle who spoke of the nine moving heavens and Dante's source is St Thomas Aquinas who quotes from Aristotle's *De coelo et mundo*.

XXIX, 15: *nine moving heavens*: According to the system of Ptolemy, there are seven heavens which bear seven planets (the moon, Mercury, Venus, the sun, Mars, Jupiter, Saturn), one heaven which bears the fixed stars, and one, the Primum Mobile, which bears no planets or stars but imparts movement to the other eight. They circle the earth in an east-to-west motion every twenty-four hours.

XXIX, 17: *according to their conjunctions*: The seven planets travel along their spheres in an independent west-to-east movement, each circling the earth in this direction at a different rate. They therefore appear at different times of the year in different positions in relation to each other and in conjunction with different fixed stars, which move, in an independent west-to-east motion, only one degree every 100 years.

XXX, 10: *my epistle*: It has not been preserved.

XXX, 15: *my closest friend ... in the vernacular*: i.e. Guido Cavalcanti, who appears to have been intimately concerned in the planning of this book, and to whom it appears to be dedicated.

XXXII, 2: *someone . . . no one was closer*: This is Beatrice's brother. Two of her brothers, Manetto and Ricovero, were adult in 1287 when their father made his will.

XXXII, 12: *some expression to my grief*: As the poem was commissioned, Dante could not give full expression to his own grief, since he wished it to convey the emotions of someone else.

XXXIV, 1: *a year was completed*: i.e. it was 19 June 1291.

XXXIV, 3: *as I sat drawing an angel on some wooden boards*: Leonardo Bruni relates in his biography that Dante was a competent artist. There are several other indications in Dante's writings of his knowledge of painting and sculpture.

XXXIV, 5: *certain men to whom respect was due*: Perhaps members of the Council of Florence; or possibly church dignitaries who might have commissioned the work he was doing.

XXXIV, 9: *Someone was present in my mind*: i.e. as he drew, he was thinking of Beatrice.

XXXIV, 11: *my work of drawing figures of angels*: His work seems to have been an extensive composition of figures of angels for he is drawing on several boards. It may have been intended for a church.

XXXIV, 15: *It has two beginnings*: Perhaps Dante had already begun the sonnet and had written the first four lines when the visit occurred, and he began again.

XXXV, 6: *a gracious lady*: This is the 'donna gentile' whose identity has been much disputed. In his philosophic treatise, *Il Convivio* (The Banquet), Dante maintains that she is the symbol of philosophy and represents her as prevailing over Beatrice in his mind. Commentators are divided on the question as to whether the 'donna gentile' was both a real person, as she seems to be in the *Vita Nuova*, and a symbol, as she is presented in the *Convivio*. She has been identified by some as Dante's wife, Gemma, the daughter of Manetto Donati; by others, with Matilda in *Purgatorio*; for still others she represents many women, collectively, loved by Dante at many periods. One interesting theory is that the passage in the *Convivio* refers to an earlier version, the *Vita Nuova* (now lost) which closed with Dante's enamourment of the 'donna gentile'. In the *Convivio* he refers to the *end* of the *Vita Nuova* ('nel fine della *Vita Nuova*') as the part in which he mentions his first sight of the 'donna gentile'. In the *Vita Nuova* as we have it, this mention occurs in chapter XXXV, that is, seven prose sections and six sonnets before the end. According to this theory, Dante later added to the *Vita Nuova* in the light of a renewed awareness of Beatrice. (See chapter XXXIX and also Introduction.)

XXXIX, 1: *the opponent of reason*: i.e. the heart, thus personified in the preceding sonnet; not, of course, the lady herself.

XXXIX, 10: *for some days*: Dante perhaps means the days during which he has suffered turmoil in his thoughts (see preceding chapter). His enamourment of the 'donna gentile' obviously lasted more than some days. The prose of chapters XXXVIII and XXXIX suggests a torment of physical desire which is not conveyed in the preceding sonnet.

XXXIX, 25: *some illnesses which people suffer*: In cases of nephritis (kidney disease) red, puffy patches appear round the eyes, similar to the effect produced by excessive weeping.

XL, 1: *at the time when many people go on pilgrimages to see the blessed image*: i.e. probably in Easter week, when the veil of St Veronica was displayed at St Peter's. This relic, on which it was believed Christ's features were imprinted when Veronica wiped the blood and sweat from His face as He passed on His way to Calvary, is mentioned again by Dante in *Paradiso* (Canto XXXI, 103–8).

XL, 5: *a road which runs almost through the centre of the city*: i.e. probably the ancient Roman road, the present Via degli Strozzi, Via degli Speziali and the Corso. In this last quarter was the house of Folco dei Portinari, the father of Beatrice.

XL, 38: The Provençal word *romen* or *romien* was applied to pilgrims from the West travelling to the Holy Land. Later it was used of pilgrims travelling to, rather than from, Rome.

XLI, 3: *their noble lineage*: Dante, who took pride in being himself well-born, was susceptible to ancient lineage in others.

XLI, 9: '*Come, gentle hearts*': i.e. the sonnet he wrote for the brother of Beatrice. (See chapter XXXII.)

XLI, 24: *the Philosopher*: i.e. Aristotle. The passage in the *Metaphysics* to which Dante refers is quoted by St Thomas Aquinas (Summa III, 45).

XLI, 31: '*beloved ladies*': Dante ends, as he began, the theme of praise of Beatrice by addressing his poetry to other women.

XLII, 1: *a marvellous vision*: This is perhaps a vision which led him to envisage Beatrice as the symbol she became in the *Divina Commedia*.

CHRONOLOGY

(From the birth of Dante to his entry into political life)★

1265, between 21 May and 21 June: Birth of Dante.

1266, January: Birth of Beatrice.

1274, traditionally 1 May: First meeting of Dante and Beatrice.

1280–82: Dante composes and circulates his earliest sonnets.

1283, 1 May: Second meeting of Dante and Beatrice.

1283, May–June: Dante's father has died by this date and Dante comes of age, at eighteen, as an orphan, according to the laws of Florence.)

1283, May–June?: Dante composes and circulates a sonnet describing a dream (the first sonnet in the *Vita Nuova*). Meeting with Guido Cavalcanti and beginning of their friendship.

1283: Dante affects love for the first screen-lady.

1284: Dante composes a *serventese* containing the names of the sixty most beautiful women in Florence.

(1284?: Marriage of Dante to Gemma Donati.)

1285?: Departure from Florence of first screen-love.

1285, Autumn: Death of a friend of Beatrice.

1285, October: Dante takes part in cavalry expedition of Florentine militia in support of Tuscan Guelfs against the Castle of Poggio di Santa Cecilia, which, roused to rebellion by the Ghibellines of Arezzo, surrendered in April 1286.

1286, April–May?: Dante pays court to the second screen-love. Beatrice snubs him.

(1289, 11 June: Dante takes part in the Battle of Campaldino against the Ghibellines of Arezzo.)

(1289, August: Dante takes part in the siege of Caprona, near Pisa.)

1289, 31 December: Death of Beatrice's father, Folco dei Portinari.

★ All events, except those in parenthesis, are mentioned in or deduced from the *Vita Nuova*. The dates are not all certain.

1290, January: Illness of Dante.

1290, 8 June: Death of Beatrice.

1290, Summer: Visit to Dante of Beatrice's brother.

1291, 8 June: First anniversary of death of Beatrice; some men of importance visit Dante as he draws figures of angels.

1292?: Dante first sees the compassionate young woman (the 'donna gentile') looking at him from a window.

1293?: Vision of Beatrice as a child.

1293, Easter?: Pilgrims pass through Florence on their way to Rome.

1293?: Vision of Beatrice in Heaven.

(1294?: Composition of the *Vita Nuova*.

1295: Dante enters political life.)

INDEX OF FIRST LINES OF POEMS

Discover more about our forthcoming books through Penguin's FREE newspaper...

Penguin
Quarterly

It's packed with:

- exciting features
- author interviews
- previews & reviews
- books from your favourite films & TV series
- exclusive competitions & much, much more...

READ MORE IN PENGUIN

In every corner of the world, on every subject under the sun, Penguin represents quality and variety – the very best in publishing today.

For complete information about books available from Penguin – including Puffins, Penguin Classics and Arkana – and how to order them, write to us at the appropriate address below. Please note that for copyright reasons the selection of books varies from country to country.

In the United Kingdom: Please write to *Dept. JC, Penguin Books Ltd, FREEPOST, West Drayton, Middlesex UB7 OBR*

If you have any difficulty in obtaining a title, please send your order with the correct money, plus ten per cent for postage and packaging, to *PO Box No. 11, West Drayton, Middlesex UB7 OBR*

In the United States: Please write to *Penguin USA Inc., 375 Hudson Street, New York, NY 10014*

In Canada: Please write to *Penguin Books Canada Ltd, 10 Alcorn Avenue, Suite 300, Toronto, Ontario M4V 3B2*

In Australia: Please write to *Penguin Books Australia Ltd, 487 Maroondah Highway, Ringwood, Victoria 3134*

In New Zealand: Please write to *Penguin Books (NZ) Ltd, 182–190 Wairau Road, Private Bag, Takapuna, Auckland 9*

In India: Please write to *Penguin Books India Pvt Ltd, 706 Eros Apartments, 56 Nehru Place, New Delhi 110 019*

In the Netherlands: Please write to *Penguin Books Netherlands B.V., Keizersgracht 231 NL–1016 DV Amsterdam*

In Germany: Please write to *Penguin Books Deutschland GmbH, Friedrichstrasse 10–12, W–6000 Frankfurt/Main 1*

In Spain: Please write to *Penguin Books S. A., C. San Bernardo 117–6° E–28015 Madrid*

In Italy: Please write to *Penguin Italia s.r.l., Via Felice Casati 20, I–20124 Milano*

In France: Please write to *Penguin France S. A., 17 rue Lejeune, F–31000 Toulouse*

In Japan: Please write to *Penguin Books Japan, Ishikiribashi Building, 2–5–4, Suido, Tokyo 112*

In Greece: Please write to *Penguin Hellas Ltd, Dimocritou 3, GR–106 71 Athens*

In South Africa: Please write to *Longman Penguin Southern Africa (Pty) Ltd, Private Bag X08, Bertsham 2013*

READ MORE IN PENGUIN

A CHOICE OF CLASSICS

Leopoldo Alas	**La Regenta**
Leon B. Alberti	**On Painting**
Ludovico Ariosto	**Orlando Furioso** (in 2 volumes)
Giovanni Boccaccio	**The Decameron**
Baldassar Castiglione	**The Book of the Courtier**
Benvenuto Cellini	**Autobiography**
Miguel de Cervantes	**Don Quixote**
	Exemplary Stories
Dante	**The Divine Comedy** (in 3 volumes)
	La Vita Nuova
Bernal Diaz	**The Conquest of New Spain**
Carlo Goldoni	**Four Comedies (The Venetian Twins/The Artful Widow/Mirandolina/The Superior Residence)**
Niccolò Machiavelli	**The Discourses**
	The Prince
Alessandro Manzoni	**The Betrothed**
Emilia Pardo Bazán	**The House of Ulloa**
Benito Pérez Galdós	**Fortunata and Jacinta**
Giorgio Vasari	**Lives of the Artists** (in 2 volumes)

and

Five Italian Renaissance Comedies
   (Machiavelli/**The Mandragola**; Ariosto/**Lena**; Aretino/**The Stablemaster**; Gl'Intronati/**The Deceived**; Guarini/**The Faithful Shepherd**)
The Poem of the Cid
Two Spanish Picaresque Novels
   (Anon/**Lazarillo de Tormes**; de Quevedo/**The Swindler**)